The Hottest Battle
Copyright 2020
CalebLott Publishing
All rights reserved
ISBN: 978-1-7320906-5-1
Cover photograph by: Lacie Slezak (Unsplash)

The Hottest Battle

By

Caleb Lott

CALEBLOTTPUBLISHING

While inspired by true events, the following is a work of fiction. Any similarities to any persons, living or dead, or to any circumstances are purely coincidental.

To Megan

. . . Set ye Uriah in the forefront of the
hottest battle, and retire from him, that
he may be smitten and die.

II Samuel 11:15
<u>King James Bible</u>

Prologue

1955

At four o'clock in the afternoon, on a Saturday, in the fall of
the year, a nineteen fifty-four, blue over yellow Chevrolet
Bel Air automobile turned off the Meridian Highway onto a
narrow, gravel trail and drove slowly over and around
potholes for a distance of about three quarters of a mile off
the black top, through the piney woods, and stopped in
front of a chain link-enclosed cemetery located adjacent to
the Corinthian Baptist Church.

The overcast skies sprinkled rain, and the wind out
of the northwest had a noticeable bite to it; nevertheless, the
man behind the wheel, whose mood matched perfectly the
dreary weather, was undeterred in his mission.

Near the back door of the fifty year old wood frame
structure that served as the sanctuary, a middle-aged white
man with a barrel chest and a head of thick, brown hair
turned off the engine, opened the door, and got out. He
carried a bouquet of white chrysanthemums in his right
hand and a small folding stool in his left. His dark slacks,
white shirt, and cordovan-colored, winged tipped brogues
were new and therefore a mismatch for the shabby jacket
that he wore, a tan barn coat that was stained on the sleeves.

The man stepped up a slight incline, through a gate
in the chain link fence; and then angled to his right about
fifteen yards until he found a plain marble headstone, away
from any other plots, some ten yards from the far corner of
the four acre-sized lot. The small stone was inscribed with a
name, the dates of birth and death, and the simple
inscription: *Loving wife and eternal companion.* It was the
headstone that she had talked of having, the one she had
described in her will – the one she wanted.

A breeze ruffled the man's hair as he stood over the
grave. He opened the stool and sat down next to the
tombstone, then laid the bouquet down with his right hand
while holding his coat together at the throat with his left.
When he sat up straight again, there were tears in his eyes.

"I sure do miss ya, honey." A sob caught in his throat. "I ain't never been this lonely before in my life." He paused again. "I, I just don't see how I'm gonna make it. I, I don't think I can."

He shut his eyes, then put his hand into his right outside jacket pocket and fingered the blue steel Colt revolver inside. The piece was cold and hard, and the man considered, just for a second, pulling it and ending his pain.

"Why'd you have ta leave me? I shoulda been the one to go first," he whined. He paused again as another sob overtook him. "Wha-what if I try to find somebody else? What'd'you think about that?"

He sat in repose for nearly thirty minutes, alternately looking down at the stone and then up and away, into the woods that surrounded the graveyard on two sides. Then he bowed his head and closed his eyes in silent benediction. When he opened them and looked up, the sky was just as bleak, the wind just as cold . . . and he was just as alone.

Chapter 1

December 1960

Sunday

Two men, hidden by shadows, stood in the alley between Chapman's Drug Store and the Hardy Furniture Company and leaned against the drug store's exterior brick wall about fifteen feet from the sidewalk that lined the east side of Fourth Street in downtown Naomi, Mississippi.

One of the men, the shorter of the two, wore a thin and frayed corduroy coat, faded jeans, and boots caked with dried mud. He smoked. The other, who was ten years younger and a foot taller than his companion, jammed his hands into the pockets of his thick, wool peacoat and rocked back and forth in unshined oxford shoes. He wore no socks.

It was close to midnight, and the streets of this small town of about three thousand were deserted. The temperature hovered just above freezing.

Naomi was representative of most small towns in Mississippi in the nineteen sixties. As the seat of county government, it was situated in north central Wilcox County and was served by the Mobile, Memphis and Missouri Railroad (the 3M Lines); a navigable river, the Missagoula; and three, two-lane, concrete highways, constructed during the Depression, which connected the town with Meridian to the north, Jackson to the west, and the Gulf Coast. Downtown was a twenty-five square block area that was about half commercial and half residential. A depressed minority neighborhood on the south side, and an industrial park to the west, near the railroad tracks, were also not atypical.

Both men were careful to remain as far out of the light cast by the street lamps as possible so as not to attract the attention of the town marshal – really more of a night watchman than a police officer; the sheriff's office handled all of the law enforcement duties in the county – who rode the streets between eleven PM and seven AM. The shorter man puffed his cigarette and flicked the ashes onto the alley's gravel floor.

"How much longer we got ta wait?" The tall man said.

"Jus' a few mo' minutes. It ain't even midnight yet."

Neither man wore a watch, so they took their prompts from the courthouse clock. They'd been standing in the alley since the eleven thirty strike, waiting for their opportunity.

The county courthouse, a venerable stone building located almost in the center of town, was constructed in 1878 and faced north, toward Washington Avenue, one block north and a half block west of the men's location. It was a gray, Greek-revival styled building with a slight Italian influence to the south portico. The sheriff's office occupied the mezzanine on both sides of a shotgun hallway that led from the exterior double doors, down the hall and descending five steps to another set of interior doors that separated the sheriff from the county offices and courtrooms in the front of the building. The jail for white males and females was located underneath, on the ground floor; and down below, the basement – called the 'dungeon' by the prisoners – was reserved for Negroes. Both men had been incarcerated several times, and they knew well the layout of the sheriff's department.

From their vantage point next to Chapman's, the two men had a clear view of the rear of the courthouse. They'd seen a Ford Sunliner automobile drive up and park directly behind the building; they'd watched as the driver exited the car and walked up the eight stone steps to the rear door; and they'd seen a light come on in the office located in the southeast corner.

"Man, it sho' is cold," the tall man said, his voice quivering.

"Yeah, well, it gonna warm up pretty quick when dat clock sound." He put his cigarette out under foot and immediately lit another.

"When we git paid?" The tall man said.

"When the job's done." He looked his companion in the eye. "Now, shut up and 'member what I tole ja."

"A'ight, a'ight. Shit."

Five minutes later, the courthouse clock struck midnight. On the fifth chime, the shorter man looked around.

"Les' go."

He motioned to his cohort, and they walked slowly toward the corner of the drug store, and into the light. He looked both ways and, seeing no one, he nodded across the street.

"Come on."

They jaywalked diagonally across the intersection and stepped up and onto the sidewalk directly behind the courthouse. At the foot of the steps, they once again stopped to reconnoiter. The shorter man nodded toward the entrance.

At the door, the shorter man produced a key from his right front pants pocket and jammed it into the lock, made a half turn to the left, and pulled open the right double door.

When they were inside, the shorter man turned and used the panic bar to very carefully and quietly pull the door closed. The hall ahead was dark, and the only sounds they heard were the muffled snores of one of the prisoners, a trusty, asleep on a cot in the hall in front of the five cells on the next floor below; and a radio playing country music, softly, to their right.

The two men stood motionless, waiting to see if they'd been discovered. Ahead on the left were the offices of the Sheriff of Wilcox County, his secretary, and the chief deputy. That door was about twenty feet ahead. To their right, ten feet forward, was the entrance to the deputy's turnout or roll call room.

Inside the turnout room was a cubbyhole with a table and a couple of chairs used by deputies to sit and write reports, and also to examine the civil papers they were tasked to serve. Adjacent to the cubbyhole was a booking station for fingerprints and photographs that was next to a door that led down two flights of stairs to the jail below.

Off the turnout room, in the southeast corner of the building, was another small office. This one belonged to the chief clerk. It was used to settle accounts, pay bills, and keep track of impounded property. There was one small window in front of the clerk's desk, but it was clothed with print curtains that the sheriff's secretary had hand-sewn herself. Next to a wooden desk was a large walk-in vault, and inside the vault was the department's arsenal: shotguns, rifles, additional handguns, as well as tear gas canisters and several sets of leg irons.

The desk was a medium-sized piece on which sat a blotter that was covered over with invoices and a ledger. A Philco brand, tabletop radio, tuned to the town's only station, was on the left side next to the 'in' 'out' and 'pending' baskets, and a telephone. A book of checks was on the other side of the desk, and a fountain pen lay beside it.

The shorter man motioned toward the turnout room. Then he reached into his inside jacket pocket and produced a hunting knife with an eight-inch blade and a rawhide handle. The tall man took his cue and pulled a ball peen hammer from his right front, pants pocket. They walked silently into the turnout room and then pointed themselves toward the clerk's office.

Standing on either side of the office door, they looked around the facing and spied a solitary man in a swivel chair seated at the desk. A banker's light with a green shade provided the only illumination. To their right, they could see that the vault door was open.

At the desk, the man was engrossed in the figures on a page in the journal that sat before him. While he thought, he twirled a yellow, number two pencil in the fingers of his right hand. The radio played softly: *Last Date*, a Floyd Cramer instrumental.

He was a white man with crew cut black hair and broad shoulders. He wore a red and blue flannel shirt, jeans, and work boots; and his leather jacket was draped over the back of his chair. Noticeably absent from his ensemble was any type of firearm.

The man with the knife looked at his accomplice and nodded. He stepped over the threshold and into the room, kicking a trashcan in the process. The man at the desk turned around with a start.

"Who are you? What are ya'll doin' here?"

"Stand up," the shorter man said.

The man rose, and as he did the tall man stepped toward him and struck him square in the forehead with the hammer. The man was stunned but did not immediately fall. The shorter man stepped up.

"Get in dat safe."

He pushed his victim forward causing him to stumble past the foot-thick vault door. The tall man stood behind him and struck him again, twice more, this time on the back of the head. The victim fell, unconscious.

The shorter man bent over him and began stabbing him in the back. Then he rolled him over and stabbed him repeatedly in the left side, until his arm hurt.

Then, it was over.

When they were satisfied that their target was dead, both men stood up straight and inspected their sin. There was blood on their clothes.

"Shit," the tall man said. He seemed surprised at his own brutality. "We sho' fucked him up."

"Le's get outta here."

They retraced their steps back out into the hall, through the back door, down the steps, and into the street. Looking all around, they saw no one. Only a cur dog that ambled down the sidewalk behind them witnessed their getaway.

Chapter 2

Monday

Margene Tyler, who was a part of the family that owned Tyler Farms – in the past a plantation that produced cotton and horses, now a soybean and catfish farm in the northeast corner of the county – unlocked the back door of the courthouse and walked into the hallway at a quarter past seven the next morning, a Monday, the last week in December.

Margene was in her mid-thirties and slim, and her mouse brown hair was cut Jackie Kennedy-style and held tight with hairspray. In addition, the gray pencil skirt and long sleeved white blouse that she wore under her gray wool coat were also at the height of style. She'd been the Sheriff's secretary for four years, since he'd been elected in 1956, and it was her custom to get to work somewhere in the neighborhood of thirty minutes to an hour earlier than everyone else.

As she walked to her office, she wondered what she was going to do for a job now that the Sheriff's term was nearing expiration; in fact, she wondered if she even wanted to work at all. Though single, her well to do family with whom she lived, as well as a healthy trust, more than provided for her needs. She had taken the secretary's position four years ago more as a favor to the Sheriff, and as kind of a hobby, than anything else. His replacement would take office on January twentieth, and after that, he would no doubt want to bring his own 'gal Friday' on board.

In Mississippi, in 1960, sheriffs were term limited and could not succeed themselves. So, after four years, Chester David 'Chet' Winston would be out; and since his entire staff was appointed, they too, most likely, would be without jobs when Stewart Nolen, the sheriff-elect, was inaugurated the third week in January.

She passed the turnout room and looked that direction to see if either of the two day shift deputies had arrived. No one was visible. The morning sounds of the jail trusty who was supposed to remain awake all night on fire watch came up through the open door next to the booking station. After his lavations, he would be fed by the café across the street, shortly before eight.

In her office, Tyler took off her coat and hung it on the tree in the corner near the chief deputy's door. Then she walked across the room to the coffee pot that sat on a warmer, on a table along the wall next to the hall door. She took the pot and washed it in a small kitchenette at the end of the hall, filled it with water, then replaced it on the hot plate and turned on the switch. Then she dipped two teaspoons of Chase and Sanborn coffee from a can next to the warmer into an institutional-style coffee mug that she had brought from home.

At her desk, the correspondence that she had failed to retire on the Friday previous stared her in the face. At first glance, it all looked completely innocuous. Among other things, there was: a sale advertisement from a tire company in nearby Meridian; a notice of the opening of a new dentist office in Naomi; and an announcement of a charity outing to be held at the city park in the first week in January. Only the power and water bills would require any real attention. She looked at each issue, then set them all aside and began to peruse the new *Look* magazine that had arrived at the office in the same bundle.

By seven-thirty the chief deputy had not arrived; and neither had the two deputies. The Sheriff, in the last few days of his term, and with it being the interim between Christmas and New Year's, was not expected in at all. The courthouse was closed, and only the fact that one prisoner was incarcerated kept everyone from working from home.

Margene Tyler closed the magazine and looked back at the stack of letters. She seemed almost transfixed by the pile, wondering if she needed to do any work at all. She didn't know Stewart Nolen, didn't know if she wanted to work for him, and didn't know if he had the slightest interest in keeping her in his employ.

Silence reigned in the office. The only sound was the bubbles from the heating of the coffee water. Tyler shut her eyes and let her chin rest on her chest. She was tired; exhausted from the holidays. She and her mother had cooked and entertained a houseful of relatives over Christmas, and though they'd been gone close to a week, she had not as of yet had time to rest and recuperate.

Her breathing was rhythmic, and she was just before nodding off when the quiet was broken by a loud scream.

"Woooooooo, lands a livin'!!!"

Tyler jumped awake and stood up. She walked out into the hallway.

"Oo hoooo!!! Have mercy!!!"

Tyler recognized the voice as that belonging to Cyrus Roosevelt, the trusty and the only prisoner in the jail downstairs.

"Cyrus. What's wrong?" She called from the hallway.

"Oooooooo, have mercy!"

Tyler started toward the voice, which sounded as if it was coming from the turnout room. She stepped through the hall door, past two tables and their accompanying chairs, and looked first to her left, then to her right.

Roosevelt had stumbled out of the clerk's office and was standing away from the threshold, his hand over his mouth, pointing toward the vault door. Tyler walked toward him then stepped past him into the office. She turned and looked toward the direction of his extended arm.

There, on the floor of the vault, lay Thad Stennis, one of the department's seven deputies. His head was bathed in blood, as was his shirt and jeans. He was supine with both arms extended.

"Oh, my word . . ." Tyler put her hand over her mouth and stood, frozen, next to Roosevelt.

They both remained that way for several seconds. Finally, Tyler stepped back.

"We, we've got to call an ambulance," she said breathlessly.

"He don't need no ambulance, Miz Margene," Roosevelt said, "he need a undertaker."

Tyler was stunned. Her knees buckled, and she sat down in one of the wooden chairs close to the office door. Roosevelt, too, stepped back and leaned against the wall. He was a short man with a thin build and a close cropped Afro.

"We, we've got to call somebody, Cyrus," Tyler said. She spoke almost in a whisper. "Go to my office and call the hospital. The number's on a paper tacked to the wall above the phone. Tell'em I said ta send a doctor over here. Tell'em one'a the deputies is hurt."

Roosevelt left and walked across the hall, and Tyler listened as he made the call.

In fifteen minutes, Doctor Alan Booth walked in the south entrance to the courthouse carrying a black leather medical bag. He was a bespectacled man with salt and pepper hair and a bit of a paunch. His black suit was cheap, and his white shirt was wrinkled.

Stepping into the turnout room, Booth's eyes fell on Tyler, as well as Roosevelt, who stood next to the stunned woman. He stopped.

"Ya'll look like you've seen a ghost," he said.

Tyler was still in the chair, her eyes wide, and her hands shaking slightly. She said nothing but pointed toward the office door.

Booth walked that direction and disappeared into the vault. In five minutes he returned. He was carrying his coat, a stethoscope was around his neck, and his hands were bloody.

"Well, he's dead. I can't do anything for him." He looked at his two complainants. "Margene, have you called Chet?"

Tyler appeared still in shock. "Oh, uh, no. I, I haven't called anyone but you."

"Well, get up and go call him. This is a homicide. He needs to get down here and run things."

Tyler rose. "H-how did he die?"

"Hard to say with so much blood. Looks like he was beat over the head and stabbed." He turned to Roosevelt. "Did you hear any shots?"

"No, suh. I was awake 'til 'bout midnight, downstairs. Then I dozed off. I ain't heard nothin'."

"Well, he doesn't look as if he's been shot."

Tyler began walking slowly to the hall doorway. She stopped to grab the frame in order to steady herself. Then she continued on across the hall to her office to call Chester Winston.

Chapter 3

It took close to thirty minutes for the Sheriff to get to the courthouse, which seemed odd since he lived only about two miles outside of downtown, at a farm off the Meridian Highway, or Mississippi State Highway 27. He pulled up in his black, 1959 Lincoln Capri and parked in a space marked 'Sheriff', next to the Sunliner, at the foot of the exterior steps.

Winston was over six feet tall, with broad shoulders and a head of brush cut, brown hair. He'd been sheriff of Wilcox County since January of '56, and though he enjoyed the office, and in the beginning it had been a challenge, he was now finding his duties somewhat cumbersome; so he was not unhappy when Stewart Nolen had been elected sheriff last November and the end of his own term had begun to come into focus.

He wore a suede leather jacket with deer hide elbow patches over a white uniform shirt, khaki work pants, and cowboy boots. A white Stetson sat on his head at an angle; not an obscene one, but one that pegged him as casual and in control. Unseen on his person was a snub-nosed Colt revolver in his front, pants pocket.

The two deputies scheduled to work the day shift, Gilmartin Toolen and Mark Ward, were waiting in the turnout room when the Sheriff arrived. They were dressed uniformly in tan shirts over brown pants and were outfitted with Sam Browne belts. Each man carried his own personal sidearm: Toolen, a Colt .45; and Ward a Model 29, Smith and Wesson revolver in a low slung, motorman's holster. Both had a shiny, gold, six-pointed star pinned above the left breast pocket of his long sleeved shirt. The Sheriff was adamant that every deputy's star be buffed to a high luster.

Winston walked into the turnout room and stopped. He stood, arms akimbo, and looked at each person. His eyes settled on Tyler.

"Peanut here yet?" Winston was talking about the Chief Deputy, Wilton Parsons.

"No, sir. Thelma said he was out feedin' the cows. She said she'd run get him, and he'd be here as soon as he could."

Winston nodded. His eyes went from one man to the other.

"You two know anything about this?"

Toolen spoke first. He was a veteran of the conflict in Korea; a tall, slim man with a crew cut and a thick accent.

"No, sir. I was on call last night, and I didn't hear a peep. I didn't even know ole' Thad was down here."

Winston looked at Ward. "What about you?"

He shook his head. Ward was short and round and had a bald head. His horn-rimmed glasses sat tight against his face. He'd come to Naomi eight months previous in order to live with his ailing mother, after serving a short stint with the Mobile, Alabama, Police Department.

"No, sir. I don't know nothin'."

Winston looked back at Tyler. "Has the Doc been in?"

"Doctor Booth has come and gone. I, I didn't know who else to call."

"Well, how 'bout Tom?"

Margene Tyler looked stunned. Her brows went up, and she swallowed. It hit her once again that Thad Stennis was dead, and that he needed the coroner. Tears began to fill her eyes.

"Sure, okay," she said softly. She rose from her seat and walked out of the door toward her office, wiping her eyes in the process.

Winston looked around. "Who found him?"

Toolen spoke. "Cyrus did, Sheriff. Cyrus Roosevelt. I've got him in a cell downstairs."

"What about that wife beater that we had down there, uh, what's his name?"

"There's nobody else, Sheriff. Judge Johnson paroled'im jus' 'fore Christmas. The place is empty 'cept for Cyrus."

Winston said, "Oh, yeah. I forgot." He bit his lip and looked around. "Well, I guess we'll just wait on Tom, then. You two hit the roads."

Twenty minutes later Thomas Boatman, a fifty-something man with thinning hair and bony fingers stepped through the back door carrying his own black leather bag. He'd been the county's coroner for five, four-year terms – there were no such restrictions on his office as there were for the sheriff. He was on call for all unattended deaths in the county, and the job had made him very well off, as he routinely used his position to solicit business for Boatman's Funeral Home, one of two such establishments in town.

Margene Tyler met him in the hall and pointed him toward the turnout room.

"Who is it?" He said.

"Thad Stennis. The doctor said he's been beaten and stabbed."

"How's his face look?" Boatman said with an eye toward an open casket funeral.

"I don't know. I didn't look that close."

Boatman nodded to his right. "Chester in there?"

"Yes, sir. Go on in."

Boatman walked into the turnout room and then toward the clerk's office. Winston was standing in the doorway.

The two men were cordial, but not the best of friends. Winston was the fifth sheriff during Boatman's tenure, and though he knew that Boatman was using his office for personal gain, he overlooked it; mostly due to the fact that in Mississippi the coroner is the only person who can arrest the sheriff, and Winston didn't want Boatman poking around in any of *his* activities; namely, those involving matters of convict labor that had helped make Winston more than affluent in his own right.

"Step outta the way, Chet. I gotta get in here."

Winston shifted aside.

Boatman walked into the vault, tried to find a spot to kneel down on the floor where there wasn't any blood, and opened up his bag. He put a stethoscope to the obviously dead man's chest, and hearing nothing, made a note of the time in a small, bound notebook.

"Time of death, is, uh," he looked at his watch, "eight forty."

"How long you think he's been gone?" Winston looked away.

Boatman felt the dead man's face and then lifted his arm. He looked around at the dried blood and shut his eyes.

"Well, rigor's present, he's cool, and this blood has coagulated. I'd say he was dead sometime around midnight." He paused and looked at Winston. "I'll take his temperature when I get him on a slab. That'll give us a better idea."

Winston cleared his throat. "Well, yeah, but, uh . . . I guess we oughta get him an autopsy, don'cha think?"

Boatman nodded. "Alright. If that's what'cha want. I'll have to call up to Meridian and get a pathologist. I know a couple up there, and I think I can get one of'em to come down on short notice."

Both men said nothing as they stood and looked down at Stennis' body. The odors of urine and feces were beginning to create an obnoxious tang in the small confined space, and Winston wrinkled his nose in distaste. Boatman walked to the phone on the clerk's desk, dialed a five-digit number, and waited.

"Yeah, Lilly? Send Lucius over to the courthouse with the hearse." He paused. "Yeah, it's Thad Stennis." He paused again. "Yeah, he was murdered. I'll tell ya more when I get there."

Boatman hung up and turned to Winston. "I'll call the doctor when I get to the office."

"Sure. You, uh . . . well, just bill the County."

Boatman nodded. He turned toward the door but stopped.

"By the way, Chet. You think you oughta call Stewart Nolen?"

Chapter 4

Chet Winston was taken aback by Boatman's suggestion. He was on his last leg as sheriff of Wilcox County, he knew that, but it hadn't occurred to him that someone else would be responsible for any new cases that were to occur in the interim between the election and the inauguration; cases that he could not clear before the end of his term. He knew when he was elected that the law limited him to four years; still in some ways it galled him that he was being turned out of office against his will. Frankly, the thought of anyone else investigating this particular case made him nervous.

"Stewart Nolen?"

"Well, yeah. Won't be long 'fore you're gone, and somebody's gonna have a murder on their hands; and it's gonna be Nolen." He paused. "You don't put somebody in jail on this thing, and he'll be stuck with it."

Winston took off his hat, ran his fingers through his hair, and stopped to think. He didn't want to make the call, but he knew he had to.

"Oh, okay. Okay, I'll call him."

"I think it'd be a good idea."

Boatman gathered his things and turned toward the door of the vault. He looked around at all the shotguns and rifles in their racks, and the pistols hanging from the walls on pegs.

"Lucius'll be here in a few minutes to take'im off your hands." He paused. "You might wanna get a picture of him or somethin'."

"Yeah. Yeah, sure."

Boatman looked down at the body and shook his head. "Shore is a shame."

Winston looked and acted a bit dazed when he got across the hall to Tyler's desk. He stopped and rubbed his face.

"Margene, call Toolen on the radio and tell him to get back in here and watch that crime scene over yonder. Then get me Stewart Nolen's phone number."

Tyler, who had been sitting, thinking about

Thad Stennis, seemed in a trance also. She nodded and began to thumb through a phone book.

In the privacy of his office, Chet Winston sat down at his desk and rubbed his face. Stennis hadn't been his favorite deputy, but still, the sight of the savagery of his murder had jolted the Sheriff.

He removed a half full bottle of bourbon and a small shot glass from the top right hand drawer of his oaken desk, and with unsteady hands he filled the glass full. Then he downed the contents in one gulp and looked at the black, rotary dial phone to his right.

Margene Tyler opened the closed door, walked into the office, and laid a small sheet of paper with Stewart Nolen's phone number down on the desk in front of the Sheriff.

"Gil Toolen's outside watchin' the door. Lucius from the funeral home isn't here yet."

Winston nodded. "Okay. Close the door on your way out."

Tyler left, and the Sheriff reached for the handset. He dialed the number and waited. Stewart Nolen answered on the third ring.

"Stewart? Chet Winston here."

"Sheriff. Good to hear from ya. I was hopin' you'd call. You know, you and me, we need ta get together."

Winston tried not to sound disgusted. "Yeah, well, sure, but, uh, well, today ain't the day for it. I gotta fill ya in on somethin'." He paused. "Uh, Tom Boatman said I needed to call ya and, well, at least notify ya." He paused again. "Look, we've had a murder."

"Mercy. Who?"

"One'a the deputies, Thad Stennis. He was killed, uh, Tom thinks it was last night about midnight."

"Where? How?"

"Here at the courthouse. He was in the office catchin' the books up 'fore time to hand 'em off to you." He paused. "Somebody come in and beat 'im over the head and stabbed him."

Both men were silent. Nolen was a veteran, but he had never seen combat, and his heart pounded with anticipation.

"What do you need me to do, Chet?"

"Well, uh . . . I reckon you can come on over and take a look. If, uh, I mean, if we don't make an arrest 'fore the twentieth, well, I guess this'll be your baby."

Nolen stopped to think. He knew that with his own inauguration approaching that he should go ahead and take action to assist in finding the killer of Thad Stennis. But he wanted to do it his own way.

"Sure. Sure. I'll see ya shortly."

Nolen hung up the phone with Winston and immediately dialed the operator.

His home being only four blocks away, on Jefferson Avenue, Nolen parked at the rear entrance to the courthouse fifteen minutes later and walked in the back door. He looked forward toward the interior courthouse doors, then to his left and right.

Nolen was a tall, square shouldered man, over six feet and with a flat stomach; and at thirty-five years of age, he was possessed of a full head of jet black hair. With his square jaw and Roman nose, he was the picture of a superhero. He slipped off his thick, wool overcoat and walked up to Toolen, who was guarding the turnout room door.

"You're deputy Toolen, aren't'cha?"

"That's right."

"Well, I'm Stewart Nolen. I'm here to help the Sheriff. I'd need to see the body."

Toolen shook his head. "I ain't heard nothin' about that." He paused. "Nobody gets in the crime scene."

Nolen stood up straight. "I need to get in and take a look at that body."

His tone was stern but not angry. He looked Toolen in the eye and wondered if this was a man he would want to retain when he set up his office.

"Not without the okay from the Sheriff."

"I just talked with him fifteen minutes ago. He called me."

"So you say."

"Well, where is he? Let's get him out here."

"No, sir. I ain't gonna bother the Sheriff. He's over in his office."

"I'll get him."

Without another word, Nolen turned and walked toward the open door on the other side of the hall. Margene Tyler looked up then stood up to meet him.

"Is the Sheriff in there?" He said nodding toward the closed door behind her desk.

"Yes, but . . ."

Nolen abruptly walked past her and through the door into Winston's office. The Sheriff, who was leaned back in his chair with his eyes closed, sat up immediately.

The office was twelve by sixteen and carpeted. The Sheriff's desk, a large executive-sized piece, sat against the west wall, and there were bookshelves against two of the other three. Black curtains dressed the only window, on the west side, almost behind the Sheriff's chair, giving the space a dark, ominous feel, even at nearly ten in the morning.

"I'm here, Sheriff," Nolen said.

Winston cleared his throat. "Yeah. So ya are."

"I wanna take a look at the body."

"Is it still here? I was told that Lucius from over at the funeral home was on his way to get it."

Nolen snorted. "Well, what have you done? Has anybody took pictures? Dusted for prints? What evidence did ya find? Has anybody told his wife?"

With that question, Winston's eyes opened wide. It was as if the most important task that he had to perform had completely slipped his mind.

"Well, uh, we're all kinda in shock around here. I, I . . ."

Winston looked away with a confused stare toward the Mississippi state flag that hung from a standard in the corner. Nolen leaned forward on the desk and looked Winston directly in the eyes. He spoke quietly but intently.

"You've got to getta hold'a yourself, Chet. There's a dead man in there – one'a your deputies. You've got to do something."

Winston licked his lips and nodded. "Yeah. Yes, uh, yeah, I do."

Nolen stood up straight again. "Let's go."

In the hall, Toolen stood aside as Winston and Nolen walked past him into the turnout room and toward the clerk's office. Nolen noticed a gurney standing just outside the office door. Clean sheets, folded neatly, lay snugly under the straps that would hold the body tight on the stretcher.

Lucius Jackson, a thin man with a short Afro, who wore a black suit that hung on him, was standing, looking, trying to decide how best to get the victim out of the vault. The smell of death was beginning to migrate out of the safe and into the turnout room.

"Wait a minute, Lucius," Nolen said.

The man froze. "Yes, suh."

"You can't take him away just yet." He looked around. "Besides, you think you're gonna move him by yourself?"

"I got Tyrone out'n the hearse. He gonna come'n he'p me when I need'im."

"Well, not now. We got things to do."

Nolen reached into the pocket of his khaki pants and took out a notebook. He started jotting down notes of everything he saw. He made a small sketch of the room, knelt next to the body, and made a sketch of it also. Then he noted the cuts and the stab wounds that he could see, after which he rose to his feet. Winston stood by and said nothing while looking down at the floor.

"How much longer ya'll gonna be?" Jackson said.

Nolen turned toward him. "You might as well go and get breakfast, Lucius, if you ain't already had it. It's gonna be a while yet."

Chapter 5

Thirty minutes later, another car pulled up to the rear of the courthouse. An overcoated man with sloping shoulders and a hat got out of black, '58 Edsel Ranger sedan and walked in the back door. He took off his gray fedora and smoothed out his thinning brown hair.

Inspector Malcolm Kent, called 'Mackey' by his friends, was the lead investigator from 'S' Troop, the State Police Barracks in Meridian, Mississippi, some thirty miles north of Naomi, in Lauderdale County. At thirty-six, he was a fifteen-year veteran of the troopers and had spent the last ten in the Bureau of Investigation.

Kent was slightly less than six feet tall, slim, with large hands and long fingers. His hair formed a widow's peak in front and was cropped short on the sides. His ears stuck out slightly, and his nose was thin and bony. A veteran of the Okinawa landing in World War II, he had scars on his right cheek and left arm to show for it. The jagged blemish on his face was the result of a hard lick by a flying piece of metal, the origin of which Kent had never been able to determine.

A Colt revolver in a cross draw holster sat in front of his left hip, and handcuffs looped over his belt in the small of his back. He recorded his notes with a Cross pen on a Spell-Write, Gregg ruled, steno pad.

In the hall, he removed his greatcoat, smoothed out his thin tie, and walked toward Toolen. He displayed his credentials and shouldered past the tall deputy into the turnout room. Looking around, he saw no one. Turning back toward Toolen, he said:

"I'm lookin' for Stew Nolen. He here?"

Toolen nodded. "He should be in the vault," he nodded toward the clerk's office, "right through that door yonder."

Kent walked that direction and found Nolen standing, surveying the body of Thad Stennis, oblivious to his surroundings.

"Stew?"

Nolen jumped. "Oh, hey, Mackey. Ya scared me. How ya doin'?"

Kent and Nolen had met at the 'new sheriff's academy,' a week-long training course put on through the state Attorney General's Office for rookie law enforcement executives. Kent had taught a couple of classes on investigations and evidence gathering, and when the two learned that they were both ex-Marines, they became fast friends. They'd spoken on the phone a couple of times since the class, and Kent had told Nolen that he would be available in the future to assist if Nolen caught a case he didn't think he could handle.

"I'm good." Kent looked down at the body. "Looks like you got a homicide on your hands."

Nolen smirked. "Yeah, well, not my hands yet."

"That's right. When's your big day?"

"January twentieth."

"What about Chet?"

"He's over in his office." He paused. "But to tell ya the truth, he looks like he's kinda out of it; like it's too big a shock for him to deal with."

"I've worked with him on a couple'a cases. He always seemed like he kept a pretty cool head before."

"Well, I don't know. Maybe those other cases were just shine killin's or somethin'; or maybe it's 'cause this is a deputy," he shook his head, "but he sure don't look up ta snuff, today."

Kent nodded. He walked toward the body and stood.

"Tell me what you've done, or what Chet's done."

"I took a couple'a pictures with my little Kodak, and I made some notes." He paused. "That's about it."

"Who all's been in here?"

"Well, me; Margene, the Sheriff's secretary; Cyrus Roosevelt, the man that found him, he's a trusty down in the jail; Gil Toolen, a deputy; Lucius, the undertaker's man; and, well, you." He paused again. "Oh, and Doctor Booth from the hospital; Tom Boatman, the coroner; and Chet. Them's the ones I know about."

He shook his head. "That'sa loada folks." He looked over his shoulder. "Is there a lock on that door?" He was talking about the chief clerk's door.

"I think so."

"Well, let's see if we can't find us a key and lock it up, so nobody else can get in." He paused and then nodded toward the Sheriff's office. "Then maybe we can get this show on the road."

In Chet Winston's office, Nolen and Kent took seats across the desk from the Sheriff, and Kent took out his pad. Winston was leaned back in his chair looking wistfully out of the now unclothed window. After saying nothing for two minutes, he turned to Kent.

"What're you doin' here, Mackey?"

Nolen spoke up. "I called him."

"What for?"

"Well, 'cause you called me, and this is gonna be my case in a few days." He paused. "And since this is a law enforcement officer that's dead, I think the State oughta handle it." He paused again. "And, well, let's face it, Chet. You don't look you've got a lotta energy left to clear this thing."

Winston's face drew up in anger. "And what makes you say that?"

"A lotta things. Number one, I hadn't seen nobody in there doing no crime scene work – no photos, no prints, no nothin'. There hadn't been any interviews conducted; and it's nearly ten o'clock and to the best'a my knowledge, nobody's even gone out and talked to Thad Stennis's widow yet."

The room was quiet. Winston looked back out the window and said nothing for a minute.

"Yeah, well, maybe you're right." He turned to Kent. "Consider this a request for assistance. You need paperwork?"

"No," Kent said. "I can do with what we have."

Winston waved his hand. "Get at it. Let me know if you need anything."

After the meeting, Kent stopped at Tyler's desk and phoned his office. As a result of that call, state crime scene personnel – Identification Officers, as they're called – were dispatched and arrived a little over twenty minutes later. Kent showed them to the office, the vault, and the body of Thad Stennis. Then he walked back across the hall to Margene Tyler's desk where he asked for and received Stennis' home address. Afterwards, he approached Nolen in the turnout room where the sheriff-elect was dutifully making more notes.

"I'm gonna go out and break the news to his wife; that is, if she hadn't already heard. You stay here and keep up with the crime scene boys. They know what to do, so it's just a matter of answerin' whatever questions they have." He paused and looked around. "Oh, and be sure and show'em that back door. The bastard that did this had to have gotten in somehow, and I didn't notice any broken windows nowhere."

Nolen nodded. "Okay. You don't need me out there?"

Kent shook his head. "No. Frankly, anything you get might taint things at a trial. I'll be doing most of the investigatin'. Your value was gettin' me in."

"Sure."

"I'll be back as soon as I can."

Kent found the Stennis residence on the far northeast corner of town, on Angle Street. It was a small, white cottage with red shutters, inside a white picket fence. The yard was neatly manicured, and lace curtains dressed the windows. The home looked perfectly idyllic.

Kent parked on the street, got out of his Ford, and walked through a small gate, up the sidewalk steps, to a red front door. He unbuttoned his black overcoat, stood to one side of the door, and pushed the bell. Looking around, he saw that the day was turning out overcast and threatening.

The small child that opened the portal was a curly haired female, about five years old, wearing multi-colored play clothes. She and Kent stared at each other for about ten seconds until finally the young girl sneezed.

"Hey, little girl," Kent said. "Is your mama home?"

The child said nothing but turned away and ran down a short hall toward the back of the small house. Kent stood in the threshold, slightly disconcerted. He had no children of his own, and, frankly, he didn't always know what to expect from them.

It took three minutes for Laura Leigh Stennis to present herself. She was a striking woman, even in jeans and a sweatshirt. Her dark brown, almost black hair, cut to shoulder length, shone in the dim light coming from inside the house; and her brown eyes, lashes, and brows drew his eyes to hers. Her hourglass figure was proportionate, her olive skin was flawless, and she had tiny hands and feet. Kent cleared his throat, reached in his pocket, and pulled out his badge and credentials.

"Excuse me, ma'am. Are you Miz Stennis? Mrs. Laura Stennis?"

"Yes. Who are you?"

He presented his badge. "I'm Inspector Kent of the State Police. I wonder if I might have a word with you."

She stared at his shield as her hand went to her throat. "Oh," was all she said.

"Please. I need to talk to you."

She nodded. "Oh, okay. Come in."

He stepped past her and into the living room. A small tow-headed boy had joined the female, and they stood in the small foyer with their mouths agape.

Kent held his hat in his hands and turned to Stennis. "I think it would be best if the young'uns – well, is there somebody that can watch'em?"

Stennis swallowed. "No, but, uh, well, they can play in the bedroom." She turned toward the children. "Benji, you and your sister go play in the bedroom. Momma's got to talk to the man." Her voice was a soft and airish soprano.

The children turned away slowly and began walking back down the hall. Kent and Stennis watched after them until they were out of sight.

"Won't you sit down?" She said.

"Thank you."

He took a seat in a club chair that faced a picture window in front. Stennis parked on a sofa on the other side of the room."

"What's this all about, Mr. Kent?"

"Ma'am do you know where your husband is?"

"Well, not specifically, no. He left here about eleven last night; said he was going to the courthouse to work on the office accounts." She looked away.

"Isn't that a little unusual? Going to the office that late at night, I mean."

"Not for him. Thad said that things were quieter, not a lot of interruptions at night; no phone calls, no radio calls, and the prisoners were all asleep." She paused. "The Sheriff leaves office in a couple of weeks, and he asked Thad to get the books balanced by then."

"What time did you expect him home?"

"Oh, well, today's his day off, and he said that when he finished in town he was going out to his uncle's farm to do some work. He was gonna sleep there last night."

Kent had taken out his pad and pen and was making notes. He noticed that she still hadn't asked him what was wrong.

"What time did you expect him back today?"

"I don't know; about four, I guess." She paused. "Has something happened to my husband?"

Kent laid his notebook on the arm of the chair. He looked Stennis directly in the eyes.

"Miz Stennis, I'm afraid I have some bad news for you." He paused. She sat up straight. "Your husband is deceased."

Her hand went to her mouth, and her eyes got wide. She began to shake slightly.

"Well, that can't be. He was just goin' out to the farm. How? When?"

"He was murdered, ma'am, last night, inside the courthouse."

Her shoulders slumped. "Oh, no." She seemed stunned, but not surprised. Kent noted the steadiness of her voice, her lack of tears, and the animation in her eyes.

"Who?"

"We don't know just yet." He picked up his pad once again. "What can you tell me about your husband?"

"Oh," she looked away and spoke slowly. "Well, we've been married since '53; and he, he's been with the Sheriff since he was elected, in '56. Before that he was an electrician." She paused. "Are you sure it's Thad?"

"Yes, ma'am. He was identified by the Sheriff." He wrote. "Was he plannin' on staying with the sheriff's office? After the twentieth, I mean."

She shook her head. "No. We, uh, I mean, he had already gotten a job with an electrical contracting company in Jackson . . . well, Canton, actually. We're in the process of selling the house, and we'll be moving."

Kent noticed that she still wasn't brimming with questions about Stennis' death. She had leaned back against the seat, and her hands lay in her lap. Her feet were together on the floor.

"Do you know of anyone that had anything to gain by your husband's death?"

"To gain? Well, no. I, I don't know. He was a deputy sheriff. He did arrest people."

"Was he workin' on anything in particular?"

She shook her head. "No. He was just anxious to get the books up to date so we could leave."

Kent wrote. "What kind of car does your husband drive?"

"We just have the one, a '59 Sunliner. Thad likes convertibles. I told him we needed something else for the winter, but that's what he wanted." She paused. "We got it down at Central Service on Jinx Avenue, downtown."

"Did he have a key to the courthouse?"

"Yes. Like I said, he often went down there late at night to work. You see, he was in the War, in Korea, and sometimes he has trouble sleepin'."

"He was in Korea?"

"Yes, sir. He was in the Army."

Kent wrote more. He didn't know exactly what to make of Laura Stennis. She seemed oddly cool at such a stressful moment. Her face betrayed no fear or anxiety regarding her and her children's future.

"Miz Stennis, if you don't mind me askin', how were things between the two of you?"

"What do you mean?" Her tone was not indignant.

"Well, were there any marital difficulties?"

She pursed her lips and shook her head. "No more than, say, you and your wife."

Kent smiled inwardly. It was not an answer.

"Who was Thad's best friend?"

Laura Stennis looked away. "Marty, I guess. Marty Morrison. He owns the TV store on Jefferson; Jefferson Avenue and Fifth Street. Marty repairs TVs."

Kent noted the information. "I guess there's only one more question, for now. Where were you last night?"

Her face was a complete blank. "Right here, with the children."

Chapter 6

Back at the courthouse, Kent checked in with the identification officers working on the crime scene. He stood in the threshold of the clerk's office and noted that Thad Stennis had been removed.

"How long's the body been gone?" he asked Barnett, a thin, middle aged man with wire rimmed glasses.

"'Bout thirty minutes. We called the funeral parlor after we got a look at him and took some pictures." He wiped the sweat from his forehead with the back of his hand.

"How'd you ID him?"

"He had a wallet in his hip pocket. And, the secretary brought over his fingerprints; they had'em on file. I matched up his right thumb."

"What about an autopsy?"

"The coroner, Boatman, said he'd called a doc in Meridian already; said he does most'a the cases down here in Naomi, and he'd take care of it."

"What's this guy's name?"

Barnett looked at a writing pad. "Compton. Jefferson Compton, a pathologist."

"Do we know anything about him?"

"I've heard his name a couple'a times. I called headquarters, and they said he was board certified." He paused. "He's comin' down this afternoon. I'll make an effort to be at the funeral home and tell him to do a full autopsy."

Kent nodded. "Tell him if there's any extra charge, the State'll pick it up." He nodded toward the vault. "What can you tell me about here?"

Barnett took a deep breath, exhaled, and looked around. "Well, it looks like he was here in the office workin' on some kind of accounting thing. There's a ledger open and a couple'a pencils out, some pencil shavins' on the blotter, and a checkbook. He had a pocket knife in his pocket with lead on the blade. I guess that's how he sharpened the pencils.

"There's blood on one'a the books, so it looks like everything started here." He nodded toward the desk. "The spatter indicates that he was prob'ly hit over the head; but there's nothin' on the floor, so I don't think he went down until he got in the vault. I found blunt force and also sharp force injuries."

"How many?"

"I stopped countin' at twenty. I think a couple were right in the heart."

"Any idea about the tool used to hit him over the head?"

Barnett shook his head. "There was too much matted blood to see a pattern. But the dents I felt were round and deep. So, I'd say it was a hammer or a wrench; maybe a tire tool."

"Any guns missin'?"

"I haven't seen an inventory, so I can't say for sure. But the chief deputy said there didn't appear to be anything gone from any of the pegs on the wall, and nothin' missin' from the long gun rack."

"How about money?"

"That secretary," he consulted his pad, "uh, Margene Tyler, says they made a deposit on Friday and there shouldn't been nothin' here."

Kent looked around as he thought of another question to ask. No money missing; no guns missing; Stennis' wallet in his pocket and his car parked outside. Robbery was not the motive.

He nodded toward the hall. "So, his wife tells me he had a key. I think we can assume that he locked himself in when he got here last night. By the way, any way to tell when he came to the office?"

"Well, the light on the desk was on, so it was after dark, I'm sure. The coroner said he thinks he was dead by twelve, so, I guess it was sometime between five and midnight."

"Can you find a point of entry?"

Barnett nodded outside. "Vaught's outside checkin' all the doors and windows, and I've looked at the back door. There's no sign of a break in." He paused. "I think Stennis would'a made sure it was locked behind him when he come in, so unless they made entry through the front of the courthouse, my guess is that whoever it was had a key."

Kent nodded. He folded his arms over his long coat and pursed his lips.

"Okay. So, let's get us a working theory." He looked at the clerk's desk. "Let's say that he got here at eleven – that's when his wife said he left home. He works 'til midnight – you turn on the radio?" he nodded that direction.

"No."

". . . plays the radio, adds up the figures, takes care of his business. Then, about midnight, he's surprised by the killer – or killers. I make it two men, don't you?"

"Two weapons, one large male victim who would be too big for a woman to handle. Yeah, I make it two men."

"They hit him over the head, but he don't go down. He stays up and tries to get to the guns." He paused and frowned. "I wonder why he wadn't wearin' his own sidearm?" He paused again. "Or, he was herded into the vault, beat down with another blow to the head, and then stabbed 'til they're sure he's dead." He paused. "Then they leave without takin' anything."

"That's as good a story as any."

Kent rubbed his hand across his face. His mind was working. This wasn't anything but an old fashioned 'hit,' he thought; purely personal.

Kent found Nolen outside, on the east side of the building, with Vaught, carrying a tape measure and holding photographic equipment for Barnett's young assistant.

"You busy, Stew?"

Nolen looked at Kent grimly. "No. We're about done here." He laid Vaught's equipment down on the sidewalk. "What's up?"

"I need to interview that trusty that found'im. Can you help me get him outta jail?"

"Sure. Let's go."

Inside, they went directly to Margene Tyler's office. They found her on the phone. Nolen cleared his throat.

"Listen, Helen, I gotta go. That investigator's here." She hung up. "What can I do for you boys?"

Nolen spoke. "We need to interview Cyrus Roosevelt. Have you got the keys to downstairs?"

She furrowed her brow. "Yes, but . . . . Well, let me see if Peanut can go with you to get'im."

She picked up the phone and dialed a two digit extension. "Chief, can you come out here?" In a second, she hung up. "He'll be here in a minute."

Wilton 'Peanut' Parsons was forty and painfully thin. Called Peanut because of the shape of his head, he was of medium height, with thinning, blond hair and leathery skin. His green eyes looked tired and not particularly alert, and it struck Kent that he was not a lawman, but merely a place holder; someone that Winston could trust to administrate but not to steal from him – or inform on him. On this day he wore his tan uniform shirt, brown pants, and work boots. The gold star pinned to his shirt was slightly tarnished, and he too, conspicuously, wore no sidearm.

"How can I help you gentlemen?" His voice was a weak baritone.

Nolen spoke. "Have you talked to Chet? About Thad Stennis, I mean."

"Yes." He shook his head. "Man, what a shock. He said there was a state investigator workin' on the case." He paused and looked at Nolen. "He didn't say nothin' about you, though."

Kent spoke up. "He's helpin' me." He paused and looked Parsons in the eye. "We'd need to talk to Cyrus, the trusty."

Parsons, appropriately humbled, nodded and said, "Let me get my keys."

Parsons escorted Roosevelt from the dungeon to the turnout room and sat him down at a table, in a chair with no arms.

He was sixty, clean shaven, balding on top, with deep lines in his cheeks and ears that protruded prominently from the side of his head. His jail clothes were white, and the word 'TRUSTY' was printed in black, block lettering above the left breast pocket and also on the back. He wore black prison shoes.

Nolen and Kent sat down across from him, and when they were settled, Parsons left the room.

Roosevelt supplied his complete full name, date of birth, and address. He said he'd been incarcerated since last September for making illegal whiskey and had been sentenced to three hundred and sixty-four days in jail.

"You musta really made that judge mad," Kent said.

Roosevelt shrugged. "I 'on't know. I guess he don't like 'shine." His voice was a mush mouthed bass.

"Do you make, or drive, or both?"

"I makes."

"You're a trusty here?"

"Yes, suh. De She'iff, he tole me when I got put in jail dat he gonna take care'a me. He say, 'jus' keep ya nose clean, Cyrus, and I'll take care'a ya.'"

"So, tell me about last night. What time d'you go'ta bed?"

"'Bout ten thutty by de co'tehouse clock."

"Did you hear anyone come in?"

"I heard Mr. Thad come in 'bout 'leben. I say, 'Dat you, Mr. Thad?' He say, 'Yeah, Cyrus. I'll be up here fo' a little while.'"

"Did Mr. Thad come down here at night very often?"

"He us'ta come jus' ever' now and then. But he started comin' a lot in the past mont'. He say he gettin' the books ready fo' the new she'iff." He nodded at Nolen.

"What happened then?"

"I read the Good Book a little bit, and den I dozed off."

"Did somebody come down and lock you up?"

"No, suh. I stays on a cot jus' at the foot'a de stairs."

"Okay, what happened after that?"

He shrugged again. "I went ta sleep. Then, when I got up this mawnin' I come upstairs ta see Miz Margene 'bout breakfas' and to see what she want me ta do today, and I look and I sees da light on in da office ove' yonder. I walked over and dat's when I seen Mr. Thad."

"What does Miss Margene usually have for you ta do?"

"I takes out da trash, sweeps da flo's, waters da plants; jus' little thangs 'round da office."

"So, after you went to sleep, you didn't hear nothin' 'til you got up this morning, is that right?"

"Yes, suh. I din' hear nothin'."

"Was there anybody down there with you?"

"No, suh. Ole man Partridge was down there 'til day 'fo Christmas. Den Judge Johnson come down and give him a parole, and he done took off." He paused. "De Judge din' tell nobody neither. He jus' done it."

"How come Judge Johnson didn't let you out? Was he the one that sentenced you?"

He nodded. "Yes, suh." He shrugged and pursed his lips. "I guess he don't hate wife beatin' as bad as he do shinnymakin'."

Kent smiled. "I guess not."

They would need to take a walk downstairs to the jail in order to look around, but at that point Kent had no reason to believe that Cyrus Roosevelt was in any way involved in Thad Stennis' murder. There was no blood on his clothes, and no one had reported seeing any; the two weapon/two perpetrator theory precluded him; and there was no apparent motive for Cyrus to have killed him. And, if he did kill him, why hadn't he escaped? And, if escape was his aim, why not just leave at any time? Roosevelt apparently had the run of the jail, anyway.

No, Kent thought, Cyrus Roosevelt had a room, a bed, and three squares. The only other thing he might would have wanted was a conjugal visit, and he could probably have gotten that, too, if he'd asked for it.

"Okay, Cyrus. There's just one other question to ask. Do you know who killed Thad Stennis?"

"No, suh."

"Who do you *think* did it?"

He shook his head once and looked down. "I 'on't know."

"Any ideas?"

He took a deep breath and exhaled. "Well, all I know is my wife done tole me a hunnert times dat she loved me, but dat she'd kill me for a silver dollar."

Kent chuckled. "Sounds like your life is pretty cheap, Cyrus."

"It do, don't it."

Parsons was summoned from his office by Nolen, and Roosevelt was escorted back to his jail cell in the dungeon.

Back upstairs, Parsons sat down at the table across from Kent and folded his hands. He looked both directions.

"You got anything yet, Mr. Kent?"

Kent looked down at his notes and feigned making more while he thought of what to tell the chief deputy. If his conclusion was correct, that someone had used a key to enter the courthouse and surprise Stennis, then anyone who had a key, or at least had access to one, was a potential suspect.

Kent shook his head. "Well, not much, yet." He paused. "What can you tell me about Thad?"

Parsons leaned back in his seat and folded his arms. "Well, he's been with us since the Sheriff got'n office. I think he was an electrician or somethin' before that. He told me that things hadn't been goin' too good for'im in that line, and he needed somethin' steady. I took a look at his background and saw that he'd been in Korea, had a lot of experience with weapons, knew how to wear a uniform and take orders and all that, so I recommended to the Sheriff that we take him on."

"You do all the hiring?"

"Well, ninety per cent of it, yeah. Sometimes the Sheriff'll come to me and tell me to put somebody on, but I'll always look into his background before we take him."

"Have ya hired anybody lately?"

Parsons shook his head slowly. "No, not lately. Mark Ward, I think, was the last man. The County upped our budget this past year, so we was able to take on another man. He come to us from Alabama."

Kent nodded. "Was Thad happy here?"

Parsons shrugged. "Yeah. Well, I guess."

"What did he do? I mean, what was his assignment?"

"Oh, well, he was like everybody else. Most days he worked a patrol shift. He also kept the Department's books; and he watched after the small arms locker."

Kent made a note. "Oh, by the way, can you take a look and see if anything's missin' from there?"

"I already did. Your man, Barnett, called me in there, and I took a look, but I didn't see nothin' gone."

Kent nodded and looked away. "Did you know that Thad was plannin' on leavin'?"

Parsons smiled. "Well, sure, we all are." He smiled and nodded toward Nolen. "Unless Mr. Nolen there wants us to stay . . . and I don't really see that happenin'."

"How'd Thad and the Sheriff get along?"

"Alright, I guess. I never noticed any problems between'em."

"Your office is right across from the Sheriff's, isn't it?"

"Yes."

"Ever hear any shouting matches about anything? Any conflicts of any sort?"

Parsons stopped to think. "No, not . . . well, there was this one time that Thad come to the see the Sheriff about the extra work he had to do, you know, with the books and all. He wanted more money."

"How'd that come out?"

"Well, they had it out in the office, but a day or so later, Chet come and told me to give'im an extra five dollars a week. So, I told the county treasurer."

Kent nodded again. "Have you ever met Miz Stennis?"

"I have. The Sheriff puts on a couple'a things ever' year: a spring bar-b-que, a Christmas party, and a fall dinner dance-type thing. They're just parties out at his farm for the employees and their families. The judges and the DA come, too. Laura came with Thad to them things ever' time we had one. She seems like a real nice lady."

"You married?"

"I am. Me'n Thelma been together for sixteen years."

"How 'bout the Sheriff?"

Parsons shook his head. "No. Well, he was. He's a widower now. His wife died back in '54."

"How?"

"Some kinda heart ailment." He paused. "He missed her for a long time, but I think he's beginnin' to get over it. He goes out to the gravesite ever' once in a while."

Kent cleaned up his notes and then looked up. Parsons sat before him with expectant eyes, and Nolen was looking around as if he was bored. Not such a good look, Kent thought, for the sheriff-elect.

"What about any'a Thad's cases? Anything that he was working on that might've rubbed somebody the wrong way?"

Parsons rubbed his face. "You know, I'll have to take a look. Seems like he hadn't had anything too big." He paused. "The County's dry, and I know he's made several moonshine cases in the past year – in fact, Cyrus Roosevelt was one'a the ones he made."

Kent's brows went up. "Did he have a co-defendant?"

"I'll have to look, I don't remember."

"What about a robbery or a murder case? He ever work on those?"

"Well, we ain't had but two or three robberies in the past year, and the Sheriff worked them; hadn't had a murder since '57. The Sheriff takes them, too."

"You think you can get me a look at Thad's cases?"

"Sure. I can have'em pulled by this afternoon."

Kent nodded as he wrote. "Okay, well, there's only one thing left to ask. Who killed Thad Stennis?"

"I wish I knew." He shook his head. "I don't know."

Chapter 7

After their meeting with Parsons, Kent and Nolen left the courthouse and walked two blocks to Momma's Café at Washington and Fifth, on the east side of downtown, for a late lunch.

Nolen found them a booth in the corner near the front window and signaled to a middle-aged woman behind the cash register. She had dark hair and a matronly figure, and her white uniform dress was splotched with ketchup in two places. The restaurant was only half full.

"Well, hey, Sheriff. We heard about Thad. We're so sorry," Margaret 'Momma' Nail said with a furrowed brow.

"Two things, Margaret. I ain't the sheriff, yet; and this is Inspector Kent from the State Police. It's his case."

Kent looked at her and gave her a half smile. She handed him a menu and put two glasses of water in front of them.

"I'll have the meat loaf plate," Nolen said. "What do you want, Mackey? I'm buyin.'"

Kent looked at the menu and found the specials. He ordered a slice of roast beef, black eyed peas, okra, and a corn muffin for eighty-five cents. It was close to one o'clock.

"I'm gonna need a place to stay tonight," Kent said. "Is that hotel across from the courthouse, the, uh, the Continental, is that place any good?"

"Sure. That's where juries are sequestered." Nolen paused and took a sip of water. "But I wisht you'd come and stay with me'n Debra. We got plenty'a room."

Kent sipped his water also. "That's very generous, but sometimes I can't sleep at night, and I get up and go walkin' or drivin' around. And I'll wanna be able to take a phone call, and if that happens late at night, I don't wanna wake up the whole house."

Nolen nodded. "What do you think so far?"

Kent took another sip. "There are some things botherin' me; namely, Thad's wife."

"What about her?"

"She just don't . . . she didn't look like it caught her by surprise that her ole man was dead. Oh, I don't think she killed him, but it wouldn't surprise me if she was behind it."

He hushed as Margaret Nail brought their two plates and set them down on the table. Kent asked for ketchup, and Nail placed a bottle down in front of him.

"I don't see why you need ketchup; not with gravy on that beef."

Kent looked at her with distaste, and she turned and walked off. He used a knife to trim a copious amount of fat off the edge of the meat but decided not to complain about a free meal.

"The thing that bothers me," Nolen said as he took a bite of meatloaf, "is Chet. Seems to me like he'd be all over this thing."

Kent pursed his lips. "You'd think. Like I said, I've worked at least two other murder cases with'im, and he was always up to the task." He paused and took a bite of bread. "Strange."

Nolen sipped his iced tea just as a high school girl
on the other side of the room put a nickel in the juke box
and played *Mack the Knife*. He looked over his shoulder in
disgust.

"So, I still remember from your class the motives
for murder: revenge, money, or love. You got any ideas
about this one?"

Kent chewed on the roast beef. "We'll know more
after we take a look at his cases. I'm particularly interested in
the one that put Cyrus Roosevelt in jail.

After lunch, Kent and Nolen walked back over to the
courthouse. Kent went to Margene Tyler's office and invited
her into the turnout room for a chat. Nolen got his car and
went home to see his wife and change clothes.

"Well," Tyler said as she sat down at the table, "I
can't stay long. There's got to be somebody over there to
answer the phone and the radio."

"Maybe Chief Parsons can take care of that for a
little while."

She frowned. "What can I he'p you with?"

"I just wanted to know about Thad; what were your
impressions of him; who you thought might wanna kill
him."

"Oh." She began to wring her hands. "Well, I didn't
know Thad too well. He, he was in and out all the time. We
never really had too much time to talk."

"What about complaints? Did anyone ever call and
complain to the Sheriff about his work?"

She thought for a minute then shook her head.
"No, not that I can remember. But I wouldn't put no stock
in that. Folks call and complain all the time and there usually
ain't nothin' to it."

"By the way? Who dispatches the department's
calls?"

"During the day, I do. I've got a radio in my office.
At night and on weekends, the telephone operator calls the
Sheriff at home. He has a base station radio at his house,
and he'll get in touch with the deputy that's workin'."

Kent nodded as she wrote. "Did Thad and the Sheriff get along? I mean, did the Sheriff ever have to dress him down?" He paused. "Did Thad always do what he was told?"

Tyler looked both ways and lowered her voice. "Well, there was a couple'a times that the two of'em got loud in the Sheriff's office. I couldn't hear what they was sayin' 'cause the sound was too muffled."

"Any ideas at all?"

She shook her head. "No."

Kent paused as if in thought. "Tyler. Are you related to the Tyler family that owns the plantation up in the north part'a the county?"

She nodded. "I am, though it ain't really a plantation no more. My daddy's brother runs the place, and he mostly raises hogs and soybeans. He's got some catfish ponds, too."

"Still, that's a pretty big spread."

"Fifty thousand acres; covers parts'a two counties. This town is named after my great, great, great, great," she smiled, "how many greats is that? Grandmother, Naomi. The Tylers was the first family in this territory back in the 1830's."

Kent nodded. "Have you ever met Thad's wife?"

"Sure. I've seen her at the get-togethers the Sheriff throws ever' year; and she's come to the office a few times to leave things for Thad and to pick up his paycheck. She seems like a real nice young lady. She's from here in town, ya know."

"I understand they were in the process of moving to Canton; he'd gotten a job over there."

"Well, that wouldn't be unusual. Once the Sheriff is outta office, the new man has the right to fire all of the employees that he wants; though I don't know how he could run the place if ever'body up and left all at once."

"Do you expect to be kept?"

"Honestly, I haven't heard."

"Would you if he asked?"

She paused. "I suppose I would, for a while. Chester and I have known each other for years, and I feel a lotta loyalty to him; but he's told me that if I want to stay on it wouldn't hurt his feelin's none."

Kent looked at his notes while thinking that Tyler staying at the sheriff's office would be a good way for Winston to keep a spy incognito.

"Tell me about the Sheriff's wife."

"Well, she died a few years back. He took it real hard in the beginnin'. Truthfully, I think her death is one of the reasons he run for sheriff; you know, just to take his mind off things." She looked away out of a window. "He loved that woman. Eva was her name."

"How'd she die?"

"Some kind'a heart problem; cardio-somethin'-opathy. She wadn't sick for very long. One day she fell out and they took her to the hospital." She shook her head and shrugged. "She never went home."

Kent nodded. "Did the Stennises look like they had any financial troubles?"

"Not that I could tell. As a matter of fact, he just bought her a new car, that Sunliner that was parked out back." She turned and looked toward the door. "I think it's gone now. Laura Leigh musta come and got it." She paused. "They gotta nice little house, and he doted on them young'uns. By all accounts, he treated her like a queen."

Kent nodded. "Okay, that's about all."

He looked down at his notes and then at his watch. It was after two.

"Oh," he said, "one more thing. Do you know if Cyrus Roosevelt's wife still lives at his address?"

She started to rise. "I guess so. I'll check his jail card in my office." She paused. "You don't think . . ."

"I don't know what I think, ma'am. I'd just like to talk to her for a minute."

"Okay. But you prob'ly won't get too much outta her. Cyrus makin' white liquor was her only means of support. The Sheriff's Office didn't do her a good turn by shuttin' him down."

Kent found Roosevelt's house in a shantytown called
Birdville, on the south side near the railroad tracks. It was
off the dead end of First Street, on Cardinal Lane.

The house was a single-story structure made of
boards that had seen better days. It had a dirt yard and a
broken down fence around the sides and back. The ringer-
type washing machine that sat on the front porch had
clothes hanging over the side of the tub, and the few
chickens that ranged about the front yard absorbed in their
scratching were surveilled by a couple of hound dogs that
lounged underneath the porch.

Kent parked his Ford on the asphalt street, did a
short hop over a drainage ditch, and walked toward the
front door while dodging dog and chicken manure. In three
long steps he was on the porch.

His knock was answered by a frail woman, middle
aged, who wore a red bandana tied around her hair. The
faded house dress she had on was held together at the neck
by one small safety pin.

"Are you Miz Roosevelt? Willie Mae Roosevelt?"

"Who is you?"

"My name's Kent, ma'am. I'm with the State
Police." He presented his badge.

"Cyrus ain't here. He in jail."

"I know. I come to see you."

"What fo'?"

"I wanna talk about the day he was arrested." He
nodded over her shoulder toward the inside of the house.
"You mind?"

She looked both ways, toward her neighbors, and
then stepped aside. Kent walked into a hot, dark living space
and looked around.

Willie Mae Roosevelt sat down on a metal folding
chair in the corner, and Kent took a seat on a spread-
covered couch near the front window. There was a wood
burning stove on the opposite wall.

"Tell me about when Cyrus was arrested. Where'd
that happen at?"

She nodded over her shoulder. "Out back."

"Does he keep his still around here?"

"No, suh. It was way down in the holler, near the slough, over tow'ds the Number 9 highway. They bus'ed it up las' fall."

"So, what'd they do? Just kick in the front door?"

She shook her head. "No, suh. Dey come on a Saturday mawnin' early and knocked on de do'. Dey didn' bus' in."

"Who told on'im?"

"I 'on't know."

"Who come out to arrest him?"

She looked up. "Well, the high She'iff come; and a white depudy wi' black hair. He was kinda tall. And they brought a black trusty 'long wid'em. He had a gun, too."

"You know who that was?"

"Antonio Lincoln."

"How do you know him?"

"He stay over on Raven Lane." She paused. "He made 'shine wid Pookie, too, sometimes."

Kent looked up in thought. "Tell me what happened. I mean, how they arrested him."

"Well, like I say, it was early mawnin'. The She'iff, he knocked on de front door and Pookie – das what I calls Cyrus – he jump up and look out the winda. He say he sees the depudy runnin' down one side a da house, so he grab his pants and took off tow'd the back do. When he got outside he was makin' fo' the chicken coop and den 'Tonio step out wid his gun pulled and the depudy say, 'Stop.' So, Pookie, he stop and raise his han's. Den 'Tonio fire off a shot wid his pistol, I guess in de air." She chuckled. "But his aim wadn' none too good, 'cause he hit de chicken house right close ta where that depudy was standin'." She paused. "Dey caught Pookie, 'cause Pookie stop when dey told him."

"What'd the Sheriff do?"

"He come around to the back when he heared the shot, and he say, 'Thad, is you alright?' And da depudy say, yeah, but Antonio like'ta kilt me." She paused. "Da She'iff ain't said nothin' else."

"The Sheriff didn't holler at him, or nothin'?"

"No, suh."

Kent nodded. He'd taken out his notebook and was in the process of making notes.

"You seen Antonio lately?"

"I seed him today; up on de co'ner. He was drunk, and I ast him where he got money to git shitfaced like dat, and he say he done did a job fo' a rich white man. I say, 'who?' And he say, 'none'a yo motherfuckin' bizness.'"

Kent pursed his lips. "Anything else?"

"No, suh. Nothin' but Pookie say he sho 'nough gotta ass whoopin' when he got ta jail. And dat judge give him a whole year to do."

"Who beat his ass?"

"Antonio."

Kent nodded. "I heard about that sentence. How come him to get so long?"

"Pookie say it was 'cause da judge and the She'iff don't like him."

Kent thought. "Okay, Miz Roosevelt, that's all the questions I got right now. You mind if come back, if I think'a somethin' else?"

"I's alright wid me. But I sho' be beholdin' to ya if you could get Pookie outta jail."

"Yeah, I heard times was hard. What are you doin' for money?"

"I went on relief. I ain't got no young'uns, so I only gets fo'ty dollars a mont'."

Kent nodded. "I'll see what I can do."

Chapter 8

As he left Birdville and rode uptown toward the courthouse, Kent thought about the case. He mostly wondered why the Sheriff was distancing himself from the investigation. He also wondered about Laura Leigh Stennis and her two children. And he wondered about the dead.

At the back door of the courthouse, he met Barnett and Vaught leaving, holding paper bags of what looked like evidence as well as all their photographic and fingerprinting paraphernalia.

"Finished?" Kent said.

"Yeah," Barnett said. He stopped and wiped his brow with the back of his hand. "I think we got about all we could."

"Anything new? I mean, other than what we talked about this morning.

Barnett shook his head. "No. I think we've got it pretty well pegged. He was sittin' at the desk, heard something behind him, turned around and got clubbed. The real beat down took place in the vault."

"You got anything we can work with?"

"Not really, no. I think you're lookin' for a regular claw hammer, maybe a ball peen; and a kitchen or a huntin' knife, with about an inch and a half wide blade. As far as prints, there was a bunch around the desk, but they're probably all the victim's. We hit everything that was metal inside the vault and come up with two latents. One of'em looked like it was somebody leanin' on a filing cabinet in order to get up." He paused. "That's about it. There was a couple'a kinky hairs that we can't compare, a blood swipe down the wall, and some back spatter on the wall above the door. I think that was from one or two of the hammer strikes."

"Kinky hair – black suspects?"

"That, or that trusty was sheddin'; or maybe the undertaker's man."

"Right." Kent nodded and made a couple of notes. He nodded toward the Sheriff's office.

"Anybody still inside?"

"Yeah, they don't go home 'til four thirty."

"Okay. Thanks. You headin' back to Meridian?"

"Yeah. We're gonna stop at the office before we knock off."

Kent left them with a wave. He found Margene Tyler in her office.

"Sheriff here?" he said.

She shook her head. "No. He left right after lunch, about one."

Kent looked away. "Don't you think that's just a little odd?"

She pursed her lips. "No. I just think he knows he's gettin' to'ard the end, and he wants to go ahead and hand it over to the next man." She paused. "Seein' death – well, I know he still misses Eva; maybe that's what's on his mind."

Kent nodded. "Can I use your phone?"

"Sure."

Kent used the phonebook to locate the number for Marty's TV and Appliance on Jefferson. He called and made arrangements to see Marty Morrison at eight the next morning.

When he hung up, he looked at Tyler.

"Where is the funeral home? The coroner's business, I mean."

"It's on Railroad Street, Railroad and First."

"Okay, thanks." He paused. "You've been a big help today."

She looked at him with sad eyes. "It's been a bad day."

Kent found the single-story parlor on the northwest corner of the intersection. The business took up two lots. It was red brick with white trim, and if you didn't know it was a mortuary, you'd bet money it was a three thousand square foot residence, owned by one of the town's prominent citizens; the postmaster, perhaps.

He parked his Ford under the canopy at the back of the building and walked through an unlocked side door. There was a punch bell on the counter in front of the office. Kent hit it twice.

"Okay, okay. I'm here," Thomas Boatman said loudly as he walked through embalming room door.

At the counter, Kent badged him. "My name's Kent, State Police."

"Oh, yeah. Stew Nolen said you'd be comin' by. We're just finishin' up in the back. Follow me."

They walked through the heavy metal door and into the fixing suite where Kent saw the corpse of Thad Stennis stretched out, nude, on a metal table. He saw the stitched up

'Y' incision made into his chest, and he saw his organs lying on a marble slab that was next to a running commode that was affixed to the wall. There was a middle-aged man with graying hair, wearing a white smock, standing over the organs, writing on a pad.

"Doctor Compton, this is Inspector Kent of the State Police."

"Doc," Kent said as he walked that direction. Compton, who looked fifty and wore glasses, glanced up but did not smile.

"I guess you wanna know all the whys and wherefores. Well, it's pretty simple, really; pretty shitty, and pretty simple."

Kent opened his note pad, while he stared down at Thad Stennis' heart.

"He was hit in the head three times with a round object; once in front, two from behind. A hammer's my best guess. Then he was stabbed eleven times in the left side, and seventeen times in the back. One of'em hit his heart. That's what killed him." He paused. "Oh, any one of'em would'a killed'im eventually, especially the head licks, but the wound to the heart took him instantly."

Kent wrote. "Anything else?"

"Well, he didn't have anything on his stomach, so it was at least eight hours since his last meal. I'm checkin' his blood for alcohol, but I didn't smell anything on'im." He paused and looked at his necropsy notes. "Why he didn't have his sidearm on is the biggest mystery to me. He might could'a got off a shot or two."

"Well, inside the courthouse, at night, behind a locked door, I guess he didn't feel like he needed any protection; especially with the gun vault right next to'im."

The truth was that Kent had been wondering the same thing. Could it be that Stennis didn't feel like an officer anymore? That since his time as a lawman was almost up he didn't feel comfortable wearing the equipment? Or was it that he didn't feel any kinship with the other officers, or with the Sheriff. Most men feel like, 'once an officer, always an officer.' Apparently, Stennis did not share that sentiment.

Compton smirked. "If you're a lawman, you need to be strapped."

Kent patted his left hip and his own revolver in the holster. "I believe in it."

"Anyway, his coronary arteries are about twenty per cent occluded; he has a tattoo of a griffin on his right deltoid; there's a scar on his leg that looks like a bullet wound; and he's missin' two toes on his right foot and one on his left."

"I wonder if that happened in the war. I heard he was in Korea."

"Well, they told me he was a vet. I didn't know where ner when. I was in the big one, myself, WW2." He paused and looked back at Stennis' body. "That's about it. It's a sad end to what I hear was a pretty good ole boy."

Kent left and found his way back to downtown Naomi. He stopped at a red light on the corner at the front of the courthouse and looked across at the three-story Continental Hotel. He half wanted to drive back to Meridian and sleep in his own bed, but he decided to get a room.

The male at the front desk was forty and thin. His spectacled face was clean shaven and bony, and the blue suit that he wore was two sizes too big. He rose from his seat at the hotel switchboard where he was reading a magazine and walked to the desk.

"Yes, sir. Can I help you?"

"I need a single; something on the third floor."

"I see. Okay, well, sign in here."

The man pointed to the registration card on the counter then turned and retrieved a key from the boxes behind him.

"Number 301, Mister, uh, Kent." He picked up the card and looked at him. "You're with the State Police, here working on Thad Stennis's case, aren't'cha?"

"News travels fast."

"Not really. You've been in town all day."

Kent picked up the 'go' bag that he kept in the trunk of his Ford for just such overnight stops as this and looked at the thin man.

"Did you know Thad Stennis, Mister, uh . . ."

"Street, Elton Street. Yeah, I knew him from the Baptist Church."

"Really? He went to church?"

"He did."

"What about the Sheriff? Where does he go?"

"Same place – well, when he goes, that is. First Baptist, a block down." He nodded to the west.

Kent leaned on the counter. "What kinda guy was Stennis?"

"He was a pretty good ole boy. I think workin' for the Sheriff took its toll on'im a little bit; seein' all that crime, I mean. He was on full time until about a month ago. Then he quit. He come back to work a week or so later, but I think it was only part time."

"Part time? He made enough to feed his family on that?"

"I don't think he needed to. See, he was gonna leave town when the Sheriff's term was up."

"You know why he quit?"

"I don't know. But I do know that about six months ago he kinda changed."

"Changed? Changed how?"

"It seemed like he got kinda moody, almost angry; like somethin' hurt his feelin's."

"Did he ever say what happened?"

"Not to me. He just wadn't the same man as before."

Kent looked at Street. "How'd Stennis and his wife get along?"

He pursed his lips. "Okay, I guess. But you know, if there was somethin' goin' on, I prob'ly couldn't tell. Folks keep things pretty well hid in a small town."

"Speakin' of things hidden, you mind if I ask you a question?"

"Sure."

"Are you a member of the Citizens Council?"

"Proudly."

"How 'bout the Sheriff."

"Well, he attends meetin's ever' now and then, but, actually, the Council is for business people only."

"What about the Klan?"

Street stared at him stonefaced. "As you well know, Mr. Kent, the Klan's membership is confidential."

"Of course." Kent gave him a knowing smile. "Okay. Well, thanks."

"You need a wakeup call?"

"No. I think I already got one."

Chapter 9

Tuesday

The next morning Kent called Nolen and made plans to meet at Morrison's Television and Appliance. After breakfast in the hotel cafe, Kent walked the short distance to the store.

He met Nolen out front, and they entered to the tinkling of a bell affixed to the door. Morrison came through a curtained doorway and stepped up to the counter.

"You must be Inspector Kent."

"I am. This is the sheriff in waiting, Stew Nolen."

"Yeah," he nodded at Nolen. "I seen you around."

Morrison was of average height but with a solid build. His blond hair was parted on the right side and held in place with Brylcreem. The leather apron around his neck covered his long sleeved, plaid shirt and dark slacks.

"Have you got a minute to talk?" Kent said.

"Sure. Anything I can do."

Kent took out his note pad. Nolen did the same.

"How is it that you know Thad Stennis?"

"We went to high school together, Meridian High. When we finished, he went off to the service, and I come down here so's I could learn about TVs; they were real new back in '50, but I kinda had a idea they was gonna take off."

He paused and shrugged. "I gotta bum knee from football, and that kept me outta the service. When old man Hackett retired, I took over his business."

"Why'd Stennis come down here to Naomi?"

"He followed his wife. She's from here."

"Just how close were you two?"

He shrugged. "We were close friends. I mean, we grew up together; played on the football team in high school, the softball team at the church; you know, went fishin', huntin', that sorta thing."

"Okay, well, tell me about him."

With that, Marty Morrison launched into a surprisingly detailed and unexpectedly succinct recitation of the biographies of Thad and Laura Leigh Stennis.

Thaddeus Leon Stennis, called Leon by his mother, and 'Thad' by everyone else since he started school, was twenty-eight years old and a veteran who'd spent his hitch in Korea with an engineering company in the 1st Battalion, 7th IR, of the 3rd Division. He saw little action until the battle and subsequent retreat from the Chosin Reservoir in North Korea where he'd been wounded.

He had grown up in Meridian but had come south in pursuit of Laura Leigh Grantham, whom he had met at a high school dance in Meridian in 1948. Called 'Leigh' by Stennis, they had dated for two years, until Stennis left to join the service. He told her that he would marry her just as soon as he returned home, which he did, albeit with three frostbitten toes and a bullet wound in his leg.

Grantham had graduated from Wilcox Consolidated High School after being voted Head Cheerleader, Homecoming Queen, Class Favorite, and the female half of the Most Attractive Couple. Afterward, she spent two years at Meridian Junior College, long enough to get a teaching certificate, and then returned home to teach first grade at Naomi School.

In '53, they were married in a small ceremony at the First Baptist Church, and Leigh supported the couple until Stennis had finished an electrician's apprenticeship in Meridian, paid for by the GI Bill. After he was established in his own contracting business, wiring houses throughout the state line area, Leigh quit teaching, and their first child, a female, was born shortly thereafter. A boy came along in '56. When Thad's business slowed, he applied for and subsequently took a job as a deputy for the newly installed Chester Winston.

Stennis had taken two years of bookkeeping in high school, and had made good grades, so Winston made him the quasi-chief clerk, and his patrol and law enforcement duties had been curtailed, but only slightly. Winston's last day in office was to be the twentieth of January 1961. Stennis's was to be the nineteenth.

Kent turned the page in his notebook. "So, what was going on in his life?"

Morrison ran his hand over his blond head. "Well, he was makin' plans to leave town. He got'im a job up in Canton, and they were gonna move just as soon as he sold his house."

"Had they found a buyer yet?"

"I don't think they'd signed the papers, but he told me that somebody'd made an offer."

"Do you know why they were leavin'?"

Morrison took a deep breath and exhaled. He hesitated and looked away.

"Look, I know you wanna know things like this, but I don't like tellin'em."

"He's gone now. It don't make no difference no more," Nolen said.

"Yeah, I know." Morrison paused, took a deep breath, and exhaled. "I think his wife had somebody on the side."

"And you know this how?" Kent said.

"'Cause Thad told me. He said he just had a feelin' that she was cheatin' on'im. I asked him with who, and he said he didn't know, but that he was gonna try to catch'er."

"Did he ever talk about divorce?"

"Never said a word. He did say that when he found out who it was, he was gonna whip his ass, and hopefully that'd be the end of it."

"He say anything about killin' whoever it was?"

"No. He said no woman was worth the gas
chamber – not even Leigh."

"Interesting. I've seen her. She's a real dish."

Morrison smirked. "Not really my taste."

"When did he tell you all this?"

"About six months ago. We was fishin' on the
Missagoula one Saturday mornin'."

"Did he tell you why he quit last month?"

Morrison shook his head. "No. It crossed my mind
that he might'a found out who it was, and that maybe it was
kinda close ta home, you know. But it may just have been
because he'd found that new job."

"How'd he feel about leavin' town?"

"Whenever he mentioned it, he acted like it didn't
mean nothin' to'im. He was just really kinda calm about it.
He did say Leigh didn't wanna leave her family."

"You ever spend much time with his wife?"

Morrison gave him the stink eye. "No more than to
say, hello." He paused. "And if you're askin' what I think
you're askin', the answer is no. I wadn't sleepin' with Thad's
wife."

A smiled crept across Kent's face. It wouldn't be
the first time a man's best friend turned out to be his wife's
lover.

"Well, I wasn't askin' that, but I'm glad you set me
straight, anyhow."

Kent and Nolen left Marty Morrison and decided to get a
cup of coffee. They walked the block and a half to
Momma's and found another booth in the corner. Kent
ordered coffee and creamed it heavily. Nolen took his black.

"What do you think about what Morrison said,"
Nolen remarked.

"You mean about Thad's wife runnin' around
on'im?"

"Yeah."

"Well, it wouldn't be the first time that a woman
found somebody that suited her better, especially one that
looks like her. She's a *real* tomato." He paused and took a
sip. "She looks like she could have whoever she wanted –

for whatever reason. But in a town this size, I don't imagine it would remain a secret for too long. There's too many eyes and ears to hide from."

"That's true. But . . ."

"So, if it is true, why haven't we heard about it before now?"

"I don't know." Nolen took a sip of coffee.

"Has Laura Leigh Stennis contacted you about anything?"

Nolen shook his head. "Haven't heard a word."

"To your knowledge, has she made any arrangements yet?"

He shook his head. "No. But, Tom Boatman would've called her yesterday. He ain't gonna let a body lay around over in his cooler for long. You'd have to know Tom, but he wants to get'em planted and get paid as quick as he can."

Kent looked away. "Any idea what the Sheriff's been doin'?"

"I haven't heard."

"I was at the courthouse yesterday afternoon and Winston had already left for the day. Margene Tyler said he took off shortly after one."

"I guess this thing's all mine, then."

"Or, ours . . . for better or worse."

At that moment, a tall, thin man wearing a white oxford shirt and dark slacks walked in the front door. His hair was brown and perfect, and black rimmed glasses sat astride his thin nose. The cordovan-colored penny loafers that sheathed his feet were shined to a high gloss.

Nolen noticed the man and raised his hand to get his attention. The tall man walked toward their booth.

"This is the Baptist preacher," Nolen told Kent. "We prob'ly need to talk to him. They usually know a lotta stuff."

Nolen rose from his seat. "Brother Walter, good to see ya."

"Hey, Stew." His voice was a mellow baritone. Both men smiled.

Nolen nodded to Kent. "This here's Malcolm Kent, Walter. He's an inspector with the State Police. Mackey, Walter Davidson." Kent nodded and took out his notebook.

Davidson nodded. "Oh, right. You're working on Thad's case." He shook his head. "Man, I don't have to tell you what a shock that was."

Nolen sat back down and slid over toward the window. "Sit down, Walter."

Davidson took a seat next to Nolen. He signaled to Margaret Nail, and she brought him a cup of coffee. Davidson added sugar to the steaming liquid, but nothing else.

"From the looks of the town, there hasn't been too much made of it," Kent said. "I mean, I haven't seen anybody at the courthouse, there aren't any wreaths; and to my knowledge, nobody's called in any tips or leads."

Davidson took a deep breath and exhaled. "Well, that could be for a couple of reasons. One, they're all in shock. Two, they don't know anything. Or, three, they're doin' all their grievin' on the inside."

Kent smiled inwardly. That was a preacher, three points and a prayer.

Davidson paused and took a sip. "I've only been at First Baptist three years, but I've found that the people here tend to keep everything hidden."

"Still . . ." Nolen said.

"There are a couple reasons why you've not gotten any leads." He shrugged. "Maybe nobody knows anything."

Kent took out his notebook. "Do you know anything about Thad Stennis, Preacher?"

"Just that he was a regular attender. He and Leigh were there 'most every Sunday with their two children."

"Was Stennis a member?"

"He was. We'd never talked about it, but from the life I saw, he appeared to be born again." He took another sip. "Leigh told me she grew up in the church. She said she was baptized back in '44." He paused and looked Kent in the eye. "How about you, Mr. Kent? Have you heard the Good News?"

Kent's mind ran to a foxhole on an island in the Pacific where commitments were made.

"I have. Thank you." He looked at his notes. "Did the two of them ever come to you for marital counseling?"

Davidson looked away. "Well, I'm not supposed to tell you if they did. But, I have heard some rumors that they were having problems. That's really all I can say."

"Well, in all those rumors that'cha heard, did anybody ever happen to mention a third party?"

The pastor shook his head. "No, and, I wouldn't have listened to them if they did. Gossip is a sin, Inspector."

Kent shook his head and smiled. "Just my luck, I get a witness with some ethics. What about the Sheriff? I heard he was a member, too. Did you ever know his wife?"

"I did not." He took a sip of coffee. "Chester Winston is not a regular attender. But I do know that he told me that when she died, he was devastated. He shared with me a couple of times that he wished that either he would find someone else – or *he* would die."

Davidson paused and took a sip. "There is one thing that I can tell you, and this wasn't a part of a counseling session. Thad told me that he'd had two very close calls in the past four months."

"Close calls?"

"At work, I mean. He said that he was almost shot trying to serve an arrest warrant out in Birdville back in September. He said a trusty accidently fired a round his direction. Then, sometime around the first week of December, he had to talk a drunk out of his shotgun, on a car stop."

"Did he say who it was?"

"No, but I think there was another deputy there. Thad said the drunk got out of the car and pointed the gun at him, and Thad was just before shooting him when the drunk got sick."

"Where?"

"Out on Number 9, right near the motel."

The wheels were turning inside Kent's head. It would probably be pretty easy to find out who the backup deputy was.

Kent nodded. He looked Davidson in the eye.

"What's the other reason?"

"What?"

"You said there were two reasons why the people hadn't called in any tips. One was that they didn't know who killed him. What was the other?"

"Oh." He shrugged and took another sip of coffee. "The other is, maybe they *do* know."

At nine thirty, Kent and Nolen walked two blocks to the courthouse. Margene Tyler was at her desk, dressed out in a subdued yet formal-looking navy blue frock with black pumps and a face full of makeup; and Parsons, the chief deputy, was in his office. Chet Winston was nowhere to be seen.

"Miz Tyler," Kent began, "I wonder if it would be possible to locate some information regarding two deputies that pulled a car over on Highway 9, near the motel; would've taken place the first week in December."

"I think so. It should be on the radio log. What kinda information do ya need?"

"Well, it was Thad Stennis on the car stop. I just need to know who, if anybody, was with him; and who, if anybody was arrested."

"Oh, well, Gil Toolen rides down in that area, so it was prob'ly him. As far as who was arrested, I'll have to look that up."

"Could you, please? I'll check with you this afternoon." Kent made a note on his pad. "In the meantime, where would I find Toolen this morning?"

"I sent him out to the industrial park to serve a notice of suit, at, uh," she looked at the notes on her desk, "Arkansas Fasteners."

"Thank ya, ma'am."

Kent and Nolen drove to the northwest side of town, past the warehouse district, and into the Bilbo Industrial Park. They spied Toolen leaving the fastener company in a marked Chevy patrol car and flashed their lights at him. He pulled over on the shoulder of Warehouse Road, and the three men got out of their cars.

"What's up?" Toolen said. He zipped up his jacket and put on his hat, a short-brimmed Stetson, against the cold wind.

Kent spoke. "We wanted to ask you if you remembered an incident on Number 9, around the first of the month, involvin' Thad Stennis pullin' a car over."

He thought for a minute and rubbed his hand across his mouth. Kent heard him click his teeth and the thought crossed his mind that what he was about to hear might be a lie.

"Oh, yeah, yeah, I remember. Thad stopped a car for speedin', out next to the motel. He called it in on the radio, and I come over there to back'im."

"Who was in the car?"

"A couple'a colored boys, uh, Antonio Lincoln; and Red, uh, Red Freeman, I think was his name."

"Did somebody pull a gun on Thad?"

"Yeah, they did." The tall man paused and put his hands in his pockets. "See, Thad didn't ride patrol a lot the last couple'a years, but this particular day Mark Ward was off doin' somethin' for the Sheriff, so Chester told Thad to check out a car and ride the south end'a the county with me. We get a lotta calls down there anyway. It was about ten in the mornin', and Thad tole me that he was drivin' by Birdville when this ole, beat up, fifty-somethin' Chevy come bustin' around the corner like a roadrunner with the runs; and so he took out after'im.

"Well, he got'im pulled over in front'a the motel down there, and the driver, Lincoln, got outta the car with a shotgun in his hand. So, Thad drew down on'im, and when I drove up, there they was, standin' out there on the road; the black boy with that shotgun, hunched over, breathin' hard, you know, like he was chokin' on somethin'."

"What about the other guy?"

"He didn't make a move 'til I got'im outta the car."

"What happened next?"

"Right after I got there, the Lincoln boy fell out on the ground. Thad got the shotgun away from'im, and the boy was callin' for his asthma medicine; a what'cha call it, an inhaler. My brother in law uses one."

"Anybody get it for him?"

"Yeah. I got this Red outta the car, handcuffed him, and then found the other one's asthma medicine on the seat. Thad dosed'im and pretty soon he come around."

"What happened then?"

"Nothin'. Thad charged him with pointin' a shotgun at'im and took him to jail. I give the keys to the car to Red and told him to get his ass back ta shantytown where he belonged 'fore I beat the shit out of'im."

Kent nodded as he wrote. "How long was Antonio in jail? Do you know?"

"It wadn't long. I think he made bond that afternoon."

"You know what Red's real name is?"

"Yeah. I think I got it in my notes. Hold on."

Toolen walked back to his squad car and opened the door. Reaching inside a briefcase on the front seat, he came out with a small, spiral notebook. He flipped pages until he found the one he wanted.

"It's Jeris. Jeris 'Red' Freeman." He recited his birth date and address and looked up. "They call him Red 'cause he's real bright – you know, complexion-wise – and 'cause his hair's red. He's got green eyes, too; real unusual for a colored person." He paused and smiled. "There must'a been a fox in the chicken house sometime 'r another."

Kent took down the information and then looked at Toolen. "You know anything about an accidental shooting over in Birdville, involvin' Thad?"

He closed his eyes and thought for a minute. "Oh, yeah. The Sheriff and Thad went out to serve a warrant and took . . . son of a bitch." He paused. "They took Antonio with'em. I 'member that at the time, he was a trusty in the jail, so they give him a gun." He paused. "I wonder why the fuck they let'im carry a piece? I wonder whose idea that was?"

Kent knew that it was not unusual for a trusty to carry a weapon when acting in the capacity of a posse member for the sheriff. He looked at Toolen.

"Gil, I'm gonna need you to keep a lid on what we talked about here today, okay?"

Toolen appeared to be in a daze when he said, "Yeah. Yeah, sure."

Kent and Nolen got in the Ford and left driving back to town. Kent had a theory. Now, he just needed evidence.

Back at the courthouse, Kent stopped in Margene Tyler's office and used the phone to call headquarters in Jackson. He checked criminal histories for Lincoln, and also Freeman.

The State Police called back in twenty minutes and allowed as to the fact that Lincoln had once done five years at Parchman Prison for Manslaughter. Freeman had one felony conviction for Burglary, when he was seventeen, but had only done a year at the county work farm outside of Naomi.

Kent took the information and walked across the hall to the turnout room where he sat down with his notes and a stack of Thad Stennis's cases to look over. It was becoming clear to him who had killed Thad, but drilling down to the motive was going to take longer.

Chapter 10

At eleven thirty, Kent stopped by Margene Tyler's office. She had the information that Kent had requested that morning.

He took out his notepad while she consulted a file. "The deputy that assisted Thad was Gil Toolen. The man that was arrested was Antonio Lincoln. He was charged with Menacing with a Firearm and No Driver's License and signed his own bond at two the afternoon he was arrested." She closed the file and laid her hands on top of it. "Anything else?"

"Yeah, a couple'a things. Who sets the bonds?"

"The Sheriff; or, if it's a felony, the Chancery Court Judge."

"When was Antonio a trusty, here at the jail?"

"Uh, well, Cyrus has been a trusty here since September. Antonio was in for bootleggin', too, and he was a trusty back in the summer before Cyrus got arrested."

Kent looked Tyler in the eye. "I need to talk to the Sheriff."

"Oh." She seemed surprised. "Oh, okay, well, he ain't in right now. I'll see if I can find him."

"Would you, please?"

Tyler rose from her desk, walked into a small room behind her and used the police radio to call the Sheriff. Kent stepped to the side of the door and listened in on the conversation.

"Base to SO 1."

"SO 1 to Base."

"Inspector Kent says he needs to talk to you."

Pause. "What does *he* want?"

"He didn't say."

Silence for thirty seconds. Then:

"SO 1, did you copy?"

"Yes, I copied," he said with disgust in his tone. "Tell him I'll be back in my office at one."

"10-4. Base out."

Tyler walked out of the radio room and opened her mouth to speak. Kent beat her to it.

"I heard. I'll see ya then."

At one that afternoon, Kent stood in the threshold of Chester Winston's office and knocked on the door frame. Winston looked up and motioned him into the room. Oddly, he was attired in a navy blue suit and red tie. Kent noted his dress but didn't comment.

"Thanks for seein' me," Kent said, as he took a seat and pulled out his notepad.

"Sure. What can I do for ya?"

"I wanted to talk about Thad Stennis. How'd you come to hire him?"

Winston cleared his throat. "Well, uh, right after I took office, I had to let about half the deputies go. I talked to'em all and there was about three that I thought didn't have the capacity to be loyal to me. You know, even though I'm limited to one term, I don't need nobody underminin' my authority." He paused. "I might want to run again in four years." He smiled slightly.

"Anyway, he come in one day and filled out a application. I took a look at it, showed it to Peanut, and a couple'a days later I called him in for a interview."

"Did he have a law enforcement background?"

"Well, no, not per say. He did say that he'd spent a little time assigned to a MP company when he was in the service." He paused. "Anyway, he was a veteran; he knew how to handle weapons; he'd had a couple'a years of bookkeepin' in high school, which I found a good use for; and he, well, he was an electrician, so he had to be pretty smart. He come off good in the interview, so I hired him. After he rode OJT with another deputy for a couple'a months, I put'im on the road."

"What about his family? Do you know them?"

"You mean his mama and daddy? No, I think they're from Meridian. And, if I'm not mistaken, his daddy's dead. It's just his maw."

"What about his wife?"

"Oh, uh, well, uh, well, yeah. I've known'er for years. She grew up around here, taught at the schoolhouse; and we go to the same church."

"Was she a regular attender?"

"Yeah, I guess. I, I don't keep that close a tab on her."

"Got any reason to believe that she's involved in her husband's death?"

He leaned forward with a furrowed brow. "What makes you ask that?"

"Well, as I'm sure you know, the spouse is always the most likely suspect."

"Oh, sure, but this bein' a particularly violent case, well, surely you don't think she come down here and stabbed her ole man ta death, do ya?"

"Oh, no. But she could'a had it done."

He raised his brows. "Maybe."

"And, there's rumors going around that maybe there was a little trouble in their marriage."

He leaned back and folded his arms. "I hadn't heard that."

"You ever talk to Leigh?"

"Sure. I, I throw a couple'a get togethers ever' year; you know, in the spring and fall, and also around the holidays. We talk then." He paused. "But I've known Leigh since she was twelve or thirteen years old. Me and my wife, Eva, we used to teach the junior high and high school Sunday School class over to the church."

"She ever mention that she wasn't happy?"

He said nothing for two beats. "Leigh? No. Uh, no."

"I understand your wife died a few years ago."

Winston looked away sadly. "She did. Eva was my first love." He shook his head. "I miss her today as much as I did six years ago when she passed."

Kent looked down and wrote. "Do you know of anybody that wanted to kill Thad?"

"No, I hadn't heard a thing."

"Sheriff, do you know a man named Antonio Lincoln?"

The question was a surprise. His brows rose, and he shifted in his chair.

"Yeah, well, sure. He's a, a regular, I guess you'd say. We've had him down here several times for whiskey makin' and drunk."

"How 'bout Red Freeman?"

"Yeah. Well, I think we've had him a couple'a times, too; seems like I sent him off for burglary right after I got in office."

"What about Lincoln? Was he ever a trusty here at the jail?"

"I think so, yeah."

"Tell me about a shooting incident that happened over in Birdville a few months ago. It involved Lincoln and

Thad tryin' to arrest Cyrus Roosevelt. You were there, too, weren't'cha?"

He chuckled. "Oh, yeah, well, ole Antonio kinda lost his head and clicked off a round in Thad's direction. He was just nervous, that's all. Thad didn't seem ta take it none too serious, and we all had a big laugh about it when we got back to the office."

"Just exactly how close to Thad did that bullet come?"

He smirked. "Oh, I don't know; three or four feet, maybe. It hit the barn or the chicken house, or somethin', way over his head."

Kent said nothing as he made more notes. Winston licked his lips.

"Are ya makin' any headway?"

Kent looked up. "We've got a couple'a leads."

"Anybody in particular?"

"Well, let's just say that we're puttin' some things together." He paused. "By the way, who's the best judge to get a search warrant from?"

"Search warrant? Well, Judge Merrill, I guess. He's pretty lenient." He paused. "Oh, don't get me wrong, you gotta have cause, but he'll give you the benefit of the doubt most'a the time."

Kent nodded. "Good to know." He rose from his chair. "I think that's all. Can we talk again?"

Winston nodded. "Sure. Let me know if I can he'p ya."

When Kent left the meeting, Tyler was gone from her desk, but he used her phone to dial Nolen's number at home. He answered on the third ring.

"Stew, I need you to go with me to Birdville. You got time?"

"Yeah, sure. I've just been goin' over deputy applications."

"Got any good ones?"

"Not too many. I think Thad gettin' killed kinda dried things up a bit."

"Too bad." Kent paused. "I'll pick you up at two."

"Okay."

It took until nearly two thirty to get Nolen and get to Birdville. They stopped on Crow Drive, next door to number fifteen, sat in the car, and waited.

Kent could see a beat-up Chevy in the driveway, and he thought about the description of the car that Toolen had given them, the car that Stennis had stopped in front of the motel the first week of the month.

"Are you loaded?" Kent said.

"Are you kiddin'? He opened his coat and displayed a forty-one magnum revolver in a leather holster."

"Okay, good. I don't anticipate any trouble, but'cha never know."

"Who are we goin' to see?"

"Red Freeman. I'm gonna try to take him back to the office and talk to him . . . but he may not wanna go."

They left the car and walked up to the front door of number fifteen. It was a wood frame, shotgun house with weathered boards, and shingles that were hanging on by a thread.

Kent knocked on the door facing and stood to one side. Nolen took the other side. A minute later the door opened.

A man who could only have been 'Red' Freeman stood in the threshold. He was close to six and a half feet tall with short red hair and a bright complexion. He wore blue jeans and a flannel shirt over a union suit, and his feet were bare. He looked no more than twenty-one

"Yes, suh."

Kent showed his credentials and identified himself. "And this is Mr. Nolen." He nodded his direction. "You Red Freeman?"

"Yes, suh."

"We need ya to come ta town and talk."

"Oh. Okay," he said hesitantly. "What we gonna do?"

"Talk."

"'Bout what?"

"Thad Stennis."

"Oh." He paused. "Well, I don't know nothin' 'bout that."

"Well, let's talk anyway. You might know more than ya think."

"Well, I ain't got no gas."

"Oh, don't worry about that. We'll give you a ride and bring you back home when we're done."

Kent reached up to take his arm, and Freeman took one step out onto the porch.

What happened next was not unexpected. Freeman wrenched his arm away from Kent's grasp and took off running toward a small pea patch that belonged to his across the road neighbor. Kent gave chase for about ten steps then drew his gun.

"Stop or I'll shoot!" Kent said.

Freeman kept running, so Kent discharged one round just above Freeman's head, and the fleeing man stopped short then stumbled forward and fell face first into the dried-up pea vines. Kent and Nolen ran to him, and Kent produced handcuffs. In a second they had their prisoner subdued.

"That was stupid, Red; just plain stupid," Kent said. His anger at having to shoot was evident in his tone.

He and Nolen lifted the tall man to his feet and walked him back to the car. It was not a quick trip, as Freeman just barely cooperated.

Nolen rode in the back seat next to Freeman, while Kent drove. They were back at the courthouse and into the turnout room in fifteen minutes.

They situated Freeman in a chair next to one of the tables and handcuffed his right hand to a leg of it. Nolen sat next to him. Kent took the seat across from him.

"Now," Kent said, "you wanna tell me why you acted like such an ass out there?"

Red Freeman swallowed but said nothing. His sullen look advertised his defiance. He looked straight ahead with knitted brows, then away, toward the floor.

Kent stood up and slapped him across the face one time, hard. "Answer me, boy." He spoke in a low but intense tone.

Freeman was shocked into attention. He rubbed his face.

"I, I was sca'ed."

"What'chu got to be scared about?"

"I, I on't know."

"Well, I do." He paused. "You recognize this room?'

The young man looked around. He looked everywhere but toward the clerk's office.

"Now, I know what'chu did, and I think I know who you did it with." He paused and pointed. "Right over there in that office . . . it was Murder."

Freeman's eyes opened wide, and he shifted nervously in his chair. His eyes darted to his left and right, but he did not speak.

"Now, I'm not gonna ask you what *you* did. All I wanna know is what Antonio did. So, start at the beginning."

Kent didn't know if it was the threat of a beating, or even that he might be killed, that affected Freeman, but the fearful look in his eyes and the tightness of his face were telling. He seemed surprised that the police had stumbled upon him and his crime, and furthermore that they were apparently willing to inflict pain in order to learn the whole truth about what all he had done.

Freeman took a deep breath and swallowed. "It was Antonio. He done it all." He paused. "He tole me that if he didn' do it, he was gonna die."

"Gonna die. He say how?"

"No, suh. He jus' say don' look for him no mo' if he didn't git it done dis time."

"This time?"

"Yes, suh."

"Okay, how'd it start?'

"He come to me las' Wednesday and aks me if I wanna make a hunnert dollars. I says, how? He say he need some back up to do a job at the co'thouse."

This time Nolen took the notes. He wrote fast.

"What happened then?"

"He tole me ta meet'im over by the drugstore on Sunday night 'bout 'leben thirty. So, I met him, and we stood in the alley and waited." He paused and licked his lips. "So when the clock strike twelve we walked 'cross the street and come in that back do' yonder." He nodded to the south side entrance to the courthouse.

"Then Antonio he creep up behind that depudy, and he whoped him over the head." Freeman looked down and to the left. "Then he commenced ta stabbin' him."

"What were you doing?"

"Man, he sho 'nough surprised the shit outta me. I jus' stood there. It su'prised me so bad I couldn't move. Dawg, man." He shook his head in disbelief.

"How'd ya'll get in the door?"

"I 'on't know. That was all Antonio."

"Didn't you watch'im open the door?"

He shook his head. "I's lookin' around, watchin'."

"Okay." Kent stopped and thought about what he wanted to do next. "What kinda clothes was you wearin' on Sunday night?"

"Uh, my wool peacoat."

"Is it at home?"

"Yes, suh."

"What was Antonio wearin'?"

He looked up in the air and shut his eyes. "Uh, some jeans and a corduroy coat, I thank."

"What about the hammer?"

"The hammer?"

"Don't answer me with a question Jeris. Where's the hammer?"

He looked down. "I buried it in the back ya'd."

"What'd you do with the money?"

"The money?"

Kent slapped him once again.

"Owww, man."

Freeman rubbed his face and furrowed his brow in disgust. He was cooperating. Why must there be additional punishment?

"I give fi'ty to my grandmamma. I done spent the res'."

Kent nodded thinking that maybe he'd gone one too far in his corporal punishment. He'd meant only to get Freeman's attention and to keep him on message; to head off any lies he might be tempted to tell. He didn't want to alienate him.

"Jeris, what happened that day out on the Number 9 highway when that deputy stopped you?"

"When?"

"You know; you and Antonio was speedin' outta shantytown in your Chevy, back around the first'a the month. Ya'll got stopped. Antonio had an asthma attack. What was that all about?"

He took a deep breath. "Oh. Well, he ain't never said, but I thank Antonio was gonna shoot the depudy then. He, uh, he jus' kinda got sick."

"Was he really sick?"

"Far as I know."

"Whose shotgun was that?"

"It was Antonio's. He got it from his daddy, I thank."

"You think Antonio tried to kill the deputy and lost his nerve?"

Freeman shrugged. "I 'on't know. Maybe."

Everyone was silent while Kent and Nolen cleaned up their notes.

"You work, Jeris?" Kent said.

"Not now. I had a job over ta the shirt factory in Lodi."

"What happened?"

"Uh, well, I got in a fight wid a white man, and they let me go."

Kent nodded. Then, Freeman spoke.

"Is I goin' ta jail?"

Kent looked at him. "You are."

"What I'm charged wid?"

"Well, right now, you're a material witness. But things change. Tomorrow it might be conspiracy."

"'Terial witness. How long can I get fo' dat?"

Kent smiled slightly. "One day . . . or a thousand years."

They worked with Freeman, without any further violence, for thirty more minutes. Then Kent turned to Nolen.

"See if you can catch Margene Tyler before she leaves. She was gone earlier."

Nolen nodded, rose from the table and walked out of the door. He was back in three minutes.

"She was at Thad's visitation after lunch, but she's back. She says she'll stay 'til you're through."

"When's the funeral?"

"Tomorrow, out at Pine Rest. There's just a graveside service, nothin' at the church."

Kent nodded. "You and I prob'ly need to take that in. You learn a lotta interesting things at a funeral."

"I'll call Debra and tell her ta get my suit out and brush it up."

"You own a suit?" Kent smiled.

"Just one."

"Okay." He paused. "Go back over to Tyler and get a phone number for a judge."

"Which one?"

"Any of'em but Judge Merrill."

It took Kent thirty minutes on Margene Tyler's Royal to tap out an affidavit in support of a search warrant for number 15 Crow Drive, and the curtilage thereabouts, detailing the fruits of the crime of the murder of Thad Stennis that Kent believed were at that location. By that time, it was dark, and serving the warrant was not possible. Kent thought about trying to get away with going there anyway, but he decided that the case would eventually become too sensitive to misplay, so he and Nolen went ahead and put Jeris Freeman in the dungeon for the night.

After they did, they went and found Cyrus Roosevelt. Kent, Nolen, and Cyrus all stood outside Freeman's cell, and Kent got right in the old man's face.

"Now, you listen to me, Cyrus. I'm gonna be sleepin' right up there next to the stairs tonight. You're gonna be in the cell right next to Red." Kent ushered him in and closed the door. "If he escapes from this jail, or if he don't live through the night, I'm gonna hold you responsible. So, if anything happens, you better wake me up." He looked at Freeman. "After all, I wouldn't want anything to happen to my star witness." He grinned slyly.

Then he turned to Nolen. "You stay here with'em 'til I get back from the Judge's house. After I get this warrant signed, I'll relieve you."

Nolen nodded. "I gotta call my wife."

"Go upstairs and do it. I'll go with ya."

Kent got out his notepad, and when he and Nolen reached Tyler's office, Kent called Judge Martin Johnson first. He got the Judge's address and told him he would meet him at his farm off the Tyler Plantation Road in twenty minutes.

Margene Tyler sat behind her desk, dumbfounded. Kent looked her direction while Nolen dialed his home.

"Margene, I," he took a deep breath and exhaled, "well, things are really pretty sensitive right now." He paused and looked her in the eye. "Can I trust you to keep all of what you've seen today a secret?"

She took a deep breath and exhaled. "Yes."

"Okay, if you'll get me a backdoor key, you can go on home. Just don't tell anyone, and I mean anyone, about what's goin' on here."

"I won't."

Her eyes were wide, and her jaw was clenched. She got a key from a ring in her desk drawer and handed it to Kent. Then she picked up her purse, put on her coat, and walked out of the Sheriff's office and into the cold Mississippi evening.

Kent found Judge Johnson's farm about three miles outside of town. He drove through the front gate and slowly up to the circular drive in front of the home's main entrance.

Inside, in the Judge's study, Johnson examined the warrant. He read slowly, and then he looked up.

"So. You have in custody a colored man that claims to have been present when Thad Stennis was killed."

"Yes, sir."

"And you want to find bloody clothes and a hammer."

"And some money, yes, sir."

Johnson, an old man of sixty-five with thinning, gray hair, took off his glasses and polished them on his dressing gown.

"I knew Thad Stennis. He worked in my courtroom many times. It's hard to believe he's dead. He was a genuinely nice man." He looked at Kent. "Why?"

"I think I know, but I don't know. This boy we've got in jail has implicated another person. It looks like whatever *they* did, they did for money."

Johnson shook his head slowly. Then he reached for his pen.

"Okay. Good luck." He scrawled his name on the page.

"Oh, and one other thing, Judge. Do you think you could revisit Cyrus Roosevelt's sentence?"

"On what grounds?"

"Well, let's just say, for humanitarian reasons; in the interest of economics. Cyrus ain't there to sell shinny, so his wife had ta go on relief."

Johnson looked up and handed Kent the warrant. "I'll think about it," he paused and smiled, "for humanitarian reasons."

"Thank ya, Judge."

Back at the courthouse, Kent used the key given to him by Tyler to let his self in the back door. He went immediately down to the dungeon to see Nolen.

"Yeah, I'm here. We just been readin' a book," Nolen said.

"Red can read?"

"No. I been readin' it to him."

Kent chuckled. "Okay. Let me make two more calls and you can go."

Upstairs, he called Barnett at home and directed him to be in Naomi at seven AM the next day in order to be present when the search warrant was executed.

Then he called the Captain of S Troop and told him he'd be staying over in Naomi for another night.

"Are you gettin' close?"

"I am, Cap, but I'm thinkin' I may need some cover on this one."

"Talk to me."

Kent shared with him his feelings about the murder and who was behind it. When he was finished, the Captain said:

"Okay. Well, just don't get your ass in a crack over this thing. If you can't tie it up tight, let it go for now. Something'll break later. They won't be able to stand it for long."

"Roger that."

Kent hung up, went back down to the jail, and lay down on an army cot that was set up behind a wall near the stairs. He was asleep in five minutes. It was eight o'clock.

Chapter 11

Wednesday

The next morning, Kent, Nolen, and a handcuffed Red Freeman met Barnett and Vaught at Freeman's house on Crow Drive in Birdville. Armed with the search warrant and a shovel, they were there to recover any accoutrements of the murder of Thad Stennis that were at the home. After they exited the Ford, Freeman gestured with manacled wrists toward the back yard.

"What are you showin' us, Red?" Kent said.

"Tha's where the hammer is, in the backyard."

They started toward the rear of the lot, and as they rounded the corner of the house, they encountered an elderly woman walking out of the back door with a wicker basket full of freshly laundered clothes. She was noticeably startled.

"Who is ya'all?" she said.

She was sixty, with graying hair and a full midriff. She wore a print house dress under a black, wool peacoat, and black US Keds with no laces. When she saw the men, she froze.

"What'chu doin' here, boy?" She said to Freeman.

"I, I gotta get somethin' for'em, Grandmama. We won't be long."

She saw the handcuffs, and her shoulders sank. "What'chu done did now, boy? Ain't I tole'ju . . ."

"I wadn't me, Grandmama. It was Antonio."

"Boy, I tole you and tole you, you better forget you ever met that sorry, no good, shif'less Negro. He ain't nothin' but trouble."

Kent pushed Freeman toward the back of the lot. "Let's get at it, Red. Where'd you say it was?"

Freeman nodded. "Over yonder, by the clothesline."

He walked that direction, stopped, and put his foot on a depressed spot in the earth. Barnett directed Vaught to begin digging, while he stood by with a thirty-five millimeter camera to record the event.

Kent left Freeman with Nolen and walked back toward the grandmother. He motioned her toward the back door.

"My name's Kent, ma'am," he said while displaying his credentials. "I'm with the State Police. What's your name?"

"Bessie Mae Tolliver."

"Miz Tolliver, is Jeris your grandson?"

"He sho is, but sometimes I wonder if he truly got my blood in him. Dat boy done been up ta some kinda devilment every single day'a his life." She paused. "He s'posed to be my own baby girl's younges', but I don't know." She paused. "His daddy be white, but he done took off," she said hoping that it might make a difference to Kent.

"Does Jeris live here?"

"Most o' the time. He stay here when he ain't got nowhere else ta go."

"Do you remember if he was here last Sunday night?"

She thought, but just for a second. "Mister, I really couldn't say. I went to chu'ch in the mawnin', den I come home and after I fixed dinner, I ain't did much'a nothin' the rest'a the day."

She paused, not wanting to implicate her grandson in anything serious. He was still, after all, her own flesh and blood.

Kent nodded and stared at the woman's coat.

"Tell me about Antonio? Has he ever been to your house?"

"He has, but I run him out jus' as quick as he git here. Dat boy'll steal the feathers off a chicken."

"Does Antonio work?"

"Psshaw. He work at not workin'."

"Did Jeris tell you what he did last Sunday night?"

"No, suh."

Red Freeman had, in fact, told his grandmother, on Monday morning, that he was at the scene of something very serious the night before. He wasn't specific, but she could tell that he was shaken. Then he gave her fifty dollars and told her to forget he had said anything.

"Miz Tolliver, is that Jeris' coat?"

She looked down at the left and right sleeves. "I 'on't know. It may be. I jus' picked up the first thang I could find to come outside and hang up the wash."

"Well, the reason I ask, is that it looks like you gotta few drops of blood on the sleeve, there." He pointed to a red substance on the left arm.

She looked at the arm, then at Kent, and quickly took off the garment and gave it to him. Kent took it, careful not to disturb the evidence on the sleeve. As he tried to fold the jacket, his attention was captured by Barnett.

"We found it." He waved to Kent.

"Excuse me, Miz Tolliver."

Kent walked to where the digging was in progress and watched as Vaught picked up a medium sized ball peen hammer. Barnett photographed it from all angles, and Vaught put it in a paper bag.

Kent turned to Freeman. "Did you bury the knife, too?"

"No, suh. 'Tonio took dat wid'im."

Inside Tolliver's home, Nolen and Kent conducted a quick survey of the interior. The appointments were old and threadbare, but clean. A black and white television sat on a small table in front of the couch.

"Where does Jeris sleep, Miz Tolliver?"

"Usually, on de couch; sometimes on de flo'."

Kent and Nolen walked over to the piece and gave it a quick once over. They located nothing of interest.

"We'll need his shoes," Kent said.

Freeman pointed toward the foot of the couch. Vaught picked them up and put them in a bag.

Kent looked around at Bessie Tolliver. "Just one other thing. Did you spend the fifty dollars that Jeris give you yet?"

"No, suh."

"I'll need that, too."

She said nothing but rose and walked into the kitchen where she removed five, ten dollar bills from a ceramic cookie jar. She thrust the cash at Kent, who directed her to Vaught and his paper bag. Kent caught sight of the first angry, then crestfallen look on her face.

Kent handed her a copy of the search warrant. "I think that'll be all, Miz Tolliver. We're sorry to have troubled you."

"I is too."

At the courthouse, as they walked into the turnout room, they met the Sheriff coming out. He froze. Kent noticed his wide eyes and watched him swallow.

"'Scuse us, Sheriff. We're just takin' Red here back to jail."

"Where've ya'll been?"

"Out."

Winston said no more. The chances were good that he didn't remember having made the acquaintance of Red Freeman. The surprised look on his face arose from the fact that he recognized that Kent and Nolen were apparently making progress. Winston could surmise that the black man they had in custody was somehow involved in Thad Stennis' murder.

"Sure," Winston said. He stood out of the way. "Uh, let me know if you need any help."

"Thank ya, sir."

They marched Red Freeman toward the stairwell door that led down into the dungeon. Kent looked over his shoulder and saw Winston watching them as they started down the steps.

When they got to the bottom, and after they'd put Freeman into his cell, Kent turned to Nolen.

"I feel funny leavin' him down here." He paused. "I'm gonna see if I can get him transferred to Lauderdale County."

"You don't think . . ."

"I don't know. I just got a funny feelin'."

Later in the morning, two gray shirted highway patrolmen driving a gray Ford Galaxie reported to the Wilcox County Jail, took custody of Red Freeman, and drove him away to Meridian. There, he was not so far away that he could not be interviewed easily, or his family could not visit him, but at the same time he was out of the custody of the friends and co-workers of the man that he had confessed to killing. Kent was satisfied.

At high noon, Kent, Nolen, and about twenty or so friends and relatives of Thad Stennis repaired to the Pine Rest Cemetery on US 38 – Baltimore Street Extension – about two miles west of town. A green tent emblazoned with 'BOATMAN FUNERAL HOME' was set up over an open grave and eight chairs, on a slight rise fifty feet west of an unpaved trail, about two hundred yards north of the highway.

The crowd was just beginning to assemble as they arrived. Nolen had gone home and changed into his suit, a gray one that fit him tight. Kent had showered at the hotel and brushed off his own clothes and hat as best he could.

The weather was overcast and gray, and while it threatened rain, precipitation was not in the forecast.

Boatman and two of his attendants (Lucius and Tyrone) were there to facilitate the event. Also, present and seated in the chairs under the tent were: Laura Leigh Stennis and her two children; an older male and female sitting on either side of her who Kent surmised were probably her parents; an older female in black who was thought to be Thad's mother, who was being ministered to by a young, blonde woman, also in black; Margene Tyler; Chester Winston; Toolen, Ward, and the department's four other uniformed deputies; Marty Morrison; and Walter Davidson. In addition, there was also one other man present: a thin, handsome, thirty-year old with blonde hair, wearing a blue suit.

Stennis wore a plain, long sleeved, black dress with a matching pillbox hat and a veil. Even in mourning, she was a knockout, Kent thought. The children were in their best Sunday clothes; the male child sporting a bow tie. Her parents were also in black, as was Margene Tyler. The Sheriff wore a gray suit and looked not the least bit perturbed by what was about to transpire.

Kent's purposes for attending were twofold: one, he wanted to see what if any emotional reaction Stennis displayed when confronted with the ultimate separation from her husband. The other was to see if there was any interaction between the widow Stennis and any other young, eligible-appearing males who might be in attendance. He and Nolen stood off to the side, out from under the tent, their posture a variation of parade rest.

"We are gathered here today," Walter Davidson said, "to mourn the passing and to celebrate the life of Thaddeus Leon Stennis, whose soul we this day commend to the hand of God the Father, through Jesus Christ the Son, by the power of the Holy Spirit."

Davidson continued with a prayer while Kent surveyed the crowd. Leigh Stennis held a lace handkerchief to her nose and sniffed quietly while on either side of her the two children fidgeted. The woman thought to be Thad's mother bowed her head and sobbed quietly into a Kleenex.

Winston stood immediately behind the chairs and rocked back and forth slowly in his brown leather cowboy boots. He held his Stetson in his hand and generally looked bored.

"Thad was a believer that Jesus Christ is the Son of God, that He died for our sins, and that He rose from the grave on the third day; and therefore we can be assured that on this day Thad is rejoicing with the angels in Heaven; seeing through a glass clearly, while learning the answers to all of life's questions and secrets; and that he has accepted his crown of righteousness for having endured to the end."

The blonde man also stood in the back, stoically, and held his hands in front of him. The thought occurred to Kent that he appeared for all the world to be a funeral crasher.

Davidson expounded for twenty minutes, in a somewhat modified eulogy, on Thad Stennis' life, his military service, his civil service, his sonship, his marital companionship, and his fatherhood. After the closing benediction, Kent and Nolen stayed apart from everyone else in order to observe.

Leigh Stennis rose from her seat and turned to her father first. She embraced him, looked him in the eye, and turned away. Then she thanked Walter Davidson with a handshake. Stennis' mother tasked herself with wrangling the two small children so that they wouldn't fall into the grave.

The blonde man was next. He stepped forward and Stennis shook hands with him. She smiled slightly, and they spoke in low tones for a moment, then the man turned and walked back toward a late model, light blue, Chevrolet Impala parked on the trail, got in, and drove away. Nolen took Kent's suggestion and walked quickly toward the road in order to take down the vehicle's license plate number.

Then Chester Winston walked forward and embraced Leigh Stennis, full on. She turned her head to the side and laid it on his chest then drew her hands to her breast in a modified pugilistic stance that Kent found extraordinary. After about ten seconds, he kissed her on the forehead and stepped away.

Stennis then turned toward the grave and watched as Boatman's men began to lower the casket into the hole. It was at that moment that she fell forward onto the top of the coffin, knocking off a rose arrangement, and began to weep uncontrollably. Her father moved quickly to her side and had to forcibly pull her to her feet and lead her away toward a black Cadillac parked at the road.

The entire proceeding lasted less than forty-five minutes.

Chapter 12

Back at the Courthouse, Nolen and Kent sat down at a wooden table in the turnout room. It was two o'clock.

"Now," Kent said. "The question is: how do we get Antonio to talk?"

"Well, he's probably left town by now."

Kent shook his head. "I don't think so. I've got a feeling that he thinks he's gonna be able to beat what he's done."

"Why's that?"

"I'll let you know later. For right now, let's go find him."

"Where to?"

"His LKA; last known address."

At three that afternoon, they drove into Birdville and found Lincoln's father's residence on Raven Lane. It was another rundown house that needed a paint job. Two dogs lay under the tall porch and there was a surprisingly well-kept flower garden on the west side near a dilapidated fence. Kent stopped and looked the place over before starting toward the steps. The hounds exited their lair and ambled toward the two men.

Kent put his foot on the second step and felt it sag. He moved quickly over it without putting his full weight down, and in a second he was on the porch. He and Nolen stood on opposite sides of the door, while Kent knocked hard on the facing.

In a minute, a short, wizened man opened the screen door and stepped out on the porch with them.

"Mr. Lincoln?" Kent said.

"Yes, suh."

"My name's Kent. I'm with the State Police. This is the new sheriff, Mr. Nolen. We're lookin' to talk to Antonio. Is he here?"

The old man looked at the ground and shook his head. "What he done now?"

"Nothin' that we know of. We think he's got some information about a case we're workin' on."

Alonzo Lincoln looked at Kent without any trace of belief in his eyes. He knew his son, and he knew that if the state police were at his house that his son had to have done something.

"Dis 'bout that moonshine thang he got hangin' over his head?"

"I'm not familiar with it. Tell me about it."

"Dey say he made some bad 'shine back las' summer, and de She'iff say it kilt three'a fo' folks. De She'iff say that after some tes's come back from the horspital that he might come git Antonio."

"The Sheriff was threatening to arrest him for manslaughter?"

"Yes, suh."

Kent knew it was not true. No lab work done last summer would take this long to complete, especially if there was a death case pending. Unless . . .

"No, sir. It ain't about that. It's about somethin' else."

"Okay, well, he *was* in de house. I'll go see can I git him up. He been out all night."

Kent and Nolen waited while Alonzo Lincoln reentered the home. They heard yelling in the background, including a female voice – no doubt Antonio's mother – and in five minutes, Antonio, sans father, stepped across the threshold and stood before them in jeans and a rumpled shirt. His hair was unpicked, and he had sleep in his eyes; but he did have boots on his feet, boots caked with mud.

"Antonio, my name's Kent, and I'm with the State Police. You gotta come on with me." He reached and took him by the arm.

"Yes, suh. No trouble, suh. No trouble atall."

"Oh," Kent said. "We need to get your corduroy coat."

"I'll git it," Alonzo Lincoln said through the screen door.

The old man receded into the house and returned in a minute with the coat. He held it out to Antonio, but Kent intercepted it.

"I'll take that."

With Kent on one side and Nolen on the other, they marched Lincoln out to the car, and all three were inside and moving in two minutes. Kent looked over his shoulder and saw that Alonzo Lincoln was watching them from the porch as they drove away, no doubt thinking, Kent believed, that he would never see his son again.

At the courthouse, all three men retired to the turnout room and sat down. Kent used handcuffs to affix Lincoln's right wrist to the chair. Lincoln asked for a cigarette, and Nolen obliged him. Then Nolen got out his notebook and pen.

Kent studied the slightly smaller than averaged-sized man and saw a confident look upon his face. His brows were raised, his head was tilted back, and he had a smirk, almost a smile, on his lips.

"Why you look so satisfied, Antonio?" Kent said.

"'Cause I know what'ch'all wanna talk about, and I know I ain't gonna be here long." Now, he *was* smiling.

"What do we wanna talk about?"

"You wanna talk about that depudy she'iff that was kilt, right over yonder." He nodded toward the clerk's office.

"And why ain't'chu gonna be here very long."

"'Cause I gotta ace."

"You do?"

"Yes, suh. I got me a ace."

Kent studied his face. Lincoln's smug look and his arrogant demeanor was galling to him. Anger welled up within him.

"Tell me about Red Freeman."

"What about him?"

Kent stood up and reached across the table and slapped Lincoln as hard as he could across his mouth sending his cigarette flying. The surprised look on Antonio's face told Kent that he had gotten the message.

"Now, you listen to me, boy. I don't know what kinda cards you think you got to play, but they don't trump what I got in my hand. I got more ways to screw you than you got fingers and toes, so you hear me and hear me good. No, more, bullshit."

Lincoln sat up straight in his chair. He rubbed his cheek with his free hand.

"Red, he stay down where I stay, on, uh, Crow, I thank."

"You and him had a deal? Last Sunday night?"

"Yes, suh."

"Tell me about it."

He looked away, as if shame, or the fear of God, or some other light had suddenly illuminated his soul. Or maybe, he was just confident that whatever he said would have no consequence, that he was protected, no matter what.

"We come in here, and, uh, Red, he, uh, he hit dat dude over the head and stobbed him 'bout a dozen times."

"How many times did you stab him?"

"I, I on't know . . . I didn't . . . once't, I thank. I don't 'member."

"Where's the knife at?"

"I thowed it away."

"Where?"

"In the Missagoula."

"What was you wearin' Sunday night?"

"Oh, uh, dat corduroy coat and some boots; and my jeans."

Kent nodded. "So, you stabbed him, once, and Jeris, he hit him over the head. Now, for the important part: How'd you get in, and why'd you do it?"

It only took Antonio Lincoln fifteen minutes to tell the truth about how this homicide was committed and at least part of why it was. Nolen took notes, and Kent did, too. When it was over, Kent rose from the table.

"Now, don't'cha feel better?"

Lincoln sat back in his chair and took a puff on another cigarette supplied to him by Nolen.

"Yeah, in a way." He paused. "But I'm still gonna play my ace."

"You're welcome to do that."

Kent looked over at Nolen and nodded to him. They both stepped outside.

"I'm gonna call the office, and we'll get him moved outta here, too. When I leave, get Parsons to put him in a cell, and you guard it." He paused and closed his steno tablet. "I've got one other interview to do." He paused. "Can you wait until the troopers get here?"

Nolen, whose face was white with disbelief, said: "Sure. Where will you be?"

"I've got to talk to Leigh Stennis." He paused. "I'll come get you when I'm through. Just hang around here and be ready to move."

Kent stopped in front of the Stennis home thirty minutes later. He took a deep breath and exhaled, and it was at that very moment that he became acutely aware of how tired he was.

It was four o'clock in the afternoon. Leigh Stennis would probably be getting ready to feed her family fried chicken, potato salad, and the other comfort foods that her neighbors had brought over to her; but Kent had already made up his mind to tell her to get the children to their grandmother's for the evening.

He knocked on the door, and in two minutes Stennis opened it. She stood before him in her black funeral dress with the sleeves pushed up; but had replaced her heels with house slippers. Her face was freshly scrubbed, and she held a high ball tumbler half full of brown liquid in her right hand.

"Well, come on in, Mister Inspector. I saw you at the funeral. What brings you here?" There was a surprised smile on her face.

Kent recognized immediately that while she was not impaired, she was very, very tipsy. That didn't take her long, he thought. Silently, he was thankful. It would make getting the truth out her much easier.

"I need to talk to you." He looked around her. "Are your children here?"

She took a sip. "Nope. They're at Mama's." She stood aside and waved her arm. "Come on in."

She followed him into the small living room, and they both took seats in club chairs on opposite sides of the room.

"I remember when you was here before. What was it, about two weeks ago?"

"Two days."

"Ha. My, how time flies." She took a sip.

Kent smiled at her convoluted logic. "But this time I've got good news," he said. He paused as she put the glass on a wooden table next to chair. "We arrested the men that killed your husband."

Her eyes got wide, and she seemed to go limp. "Who?"

"Two black men from Birdville. I'm sure you don't know them – or do you."

She swallowed. "Why'd they do it?"

He looked at her, hard. "I think you can tell me that."

She said nothing. He saw her swallow again.

"Miz Stennis, stop it. I know you didn't tell me the whole story the last time I was here." He paused. "This time, I'm not leaving without it."

She picked up the glass and took another sip. Then she held it out toward him.

"Can I get you something?"

"Just the truth."

She took a deep breath, exhaled, smirked, and raised her brows. "He wants me. He's made passes at me for . . . well, for fifteen years, really. I told him, 'no,' but he wouldn't stop."

"Who?"

"The Sheriff."

"You're gonna have to say his name."

"Chester. Sheriff Chester David Winston." There was a sneer in her voice.

"Did you ever . . .?"

She furrowed her brows. "Are you kiddin'? That pig? No. And I told him, no," she shook her head, "but he just wouldn't leave me alone."

Kent got out his notepad. "When did it start?"

"Really start? Well, I been knowin' Chester Winston since I's a little girl. He ran a hardware store downtown, and I used ta go there with my daddy on Saturday mornin's . . . you know, just ta be with daddy. Then his wife taught me in Sunday School in junior high, and we had a few parties out at their farm. When we did, he'd always come over and give me a big hug; full on, you know? Not just puttin' his arm around my shoulders. He'd face me up and rub against me and stand behind me and rub up and down my arms and massage my shoulders. It made me feel real funny . . . and kinda dirty, sometimes.

"I didn't run into him as often when I got ta high school and was datin' around; but whenever I did, he'd give me that same kinda hug. Then I met Thad. When he got back from the service, and we got married, I didn't see Chester as much." She took another sip.

Kent wrote quickly. Interesting, he thought, after all these years, Leigh Stennis is still referring to her molester by his first name.

She shrugged. "Then when Thad's electrician business started to get slow, and we had the kids, he had to look around for somethin' else to do. That's when he went ta work for Chester, right after the 'lection.

"I didn't want him to, and I told him so. He wanted to know why, but . . . I just couldn't say. I guess I was too embarrassed. 'Sides, I was afraid that Thad'd think I was askin' for it; like I was a flirt, or a tease, or somethin'.

"We needed the money, and Thad said that the job was all he could find real quick, and he didn't wanna borry from his mama . . . so, he went to work as a deputy.

She looked away. "Chester, he'd throw these bar-b-ques every spring and fall, and when we'd go, he'd always come over and hug on me, and tell me how pretty he thought I was; and he'd stand behind me and whisper in my ear how life'd be so much easier for me if I'd getta divorce." She paused. "I told him I wadn't leavin' my husband for nobody, but he kept tryin' and eggin' me on. One time, last summer, he pinched me on my hind end."

"What'd you do?"

"Nothin'. It surprised me so bad I . . . and there wadn't nobody around to see it." She paused and looked away. "Finally, I told Thad about it."

"When?"

"November – Thanksgivin'."

After four years. "What'd he say?"

"Well, he called Chester over here to the house one ev'nin' and told'im off; said that if he ever put his hands on me again he'd kill'im – sheriff or no sheriff. Then Thad backhand slapped him two or three times across the mouth and told him to get out and not to ever set foot in this house again." She took a sip.

"Then what happened?"

"Well, then Thad quit, and he went up to Jackson and found him another job." She hiccoughed. "It only took'im one day. A couple'a nights later Chester called up here real sweet and nice like and told Thad how sorry he was and to at least come back to work part-time and balance the books 'fore the end of his term." She paused. "He promised to leave me alone."

"Did you hear that conversation?"

"Yeah. I was listenin' in on the extension in the bedroom." She took another sip of her drink. "So, then, Thad went back to work . . . but it didn't help. Whenever Thad was at work, Chester'd call me. One day, right 'fore Christmas, Chester come by here and . . . well, he walked right in the front door without even knockin', just like he lived here. He told me he was gonna kill Thad, and that when he did, we could be together."

"What did you say?"

"What could I say? I just stood there with my mouth open, and he turned around and walked out." She paused. "Then when you come by here and told me about Thad . . . I, I guess I knew what happened."

"Did you warn Thad?"

"No." She looked down in silence, and her guilt and shame were made manifest.

At that moment, the thought occurred to Kent that all the attention showered on her by Chet Winston may have been flattering to her; and that the fact that there were two men willing to kill for her made her feel so wanted and attractive, and fed her ego so full, that she couldn't have divulged what she knew even if she'd wanted to. Kent marveled that a woman as physically attractive as Laura Leigh Stennis, someone who had no doubt been as affirmed as she in her past had been, still might very well harbor an enormous amount of insecurity. Deep inside, at a place that even Leigh Stennis herself couldn't locate, she loved the feeling of power that Winston's adoration and Thad Stennis' chivalry and jealousy brought her, and she felt the need to hold onto it for as long as she could; and that's why she didn't warn her husband, or even tell Kent about the Sheriff's threat after Thad Stennis was killed.

Or, maybe she just wanted herself a new man.

Only when Stennis found herself with her husband dead and her marriage bed empty, and only when she realized that her only immediate alternative had become Chester Winston, had she been shaken back into reality. That would certainly explain the paroxysm of emotion that she had displayed at Thad's funeral; the outburst that was only arrested by her father's firm hand.

"Why didn't you tell *me*?"

She shrugged. "I, I don't know. Part'a me was scared. If he killed Thad, he might kill me, too, or my babies. And, part'a me just couldn't believe that he'd really done it."

She paused. "Did, did he hire these two colored boys to kill Thad?"

"Looks like it."

She shook her head slowly. "I didn't believe he'd really do it."

Kent nodded. "Well, he did."

Chapter 13

Kent picked Stewart Nolen up at the courthouse door and pointed the car toward the Meridian Highway. It was six o'clock and dark.

"Did you get Antonio Lincoln off all right?" Kent said.

"Yeah. The troopers came and got him about a hour after you left."

Kent nodded as they drove on in silence. He was tired, but he wanted to get this case wrapped up that night and spend the evening at home, in his own bed.

"When we get out here, I don't know what's gonna happen. He might tell us to go fuck ourselves; he might break down; or he might get a piece and try to end it all – one way or another." He looked at Nolen. "You got your revolver?"

He patted his right hip. "Always."

"Alright. Just be ready for anything." He paused. "Does anybody live up here with him?"

"Not in the house; not since his wife died. I think he's got a hired man; a black fella and his family that live in a cabin, out back."

"Okay." He paused. "Will this all go down peaceful?"

Nolen swallowed. "I don't know."

About two miles outside of Naomi, they turned off the highway, drove under a brick arch labeled, 'Evaland,' and made their way slowly up a quarter mile gravel drive toward a sprawling wood frame house, painted white, with four pillars holding up an expansive porch that ran the length of the front side of the residence.

Kent parked on the circular drive, and both men got out. They walked up on the porch, and Kent was just about to engage the lion's head knocker when the door opened.

Chester Winston stood before them in an untucked flannel shirt and blue jeans. His feet were bare. Kent could see the twinkling lights of a Christmas tree behind him.

"Get out an' come in, get out an' come in," Winston said in a booming voice. His joviality indicated that he himself had consumed a toddy – or several.

"Thank ya, Sheriff," Kent said. Knowing what he knew, Winston's attitude was irksome.

They followed him into the warm house. Nolen closed the door behind them, and they walked past the Christmas tree and into an equally warm study at the back of the home.

"Ya'll take a seat," Winston said gesturing toward two cushioned chairs. He sat down behind a large maple desk.

Everyone got settled. "I guess ya'll are here to talk about the case," Winston said as he leaned back, interlaced his fingers, and laid them on his chest above his abdominal bulge.

"Yes, sir," Kent said. "I just wanted to let you know that we've arrested two of the three men responsible for killing your deputy."

"Lincoln and Freeman."

"Right. And, I guess you know most of what I'm about to tell you."

"I have my informants."

"We've only got a couple'a loose ends to clean up."

Winston nodded. "I presume that Lincoln has confessed."

"He has."

"Did he tell you . . . everything?"

Kent watched as Winston leaned forward and nonchalantly opened the righthand desk drawer. This was exactly what Kent didn't want to happen. He unbuttoned his coat thereby exposing his Colt Detective Special revolver.

"Yes, he did." Kent paused and nodded toward the drawer. "Don't even think about it, Chet."

Winston sat back in his chair, took a deep breath, and exhaled.

"Well, everything he told you was a lie. If he said I got him to kill Stennis, that ain't the truth. What he may or may not have done to curry favor with me, well, that's on him. I didn't force him or threaten him to do nothin'. Antonio Lincoln is a troubled boy who has some serious legal problems hangin' over his head. He's lookin' at a murder charge over some poison shinny."

His words hung in the air. Kent wanted him to continue, to keep talking, just as he'd want any suspect to do the same.

Winston saw Nolen looking around the room. "Ya'll like my house? Eva decorated most of it." He shook his head. "I love this place . . . but it sure is lonely 'round here, now that my Eva's gone." He waved his arm toward the patio door. "When she died, I was so bad off . . . I, I thought I was gonna die myself."

"Sure, Chet. But Leigh Stennis? I mean, what are you, twenty-five years older than her?"

He leaned forward with furrowed brows. "What did she tell ya?"

"I think 'pig' was the word she used."

Nolen snorted. Winston pursed his lips and sat back in his chair, but said nothing.

"I need to hear it from you, Chet," Kent said.

He tilted his head back and looked away. "Look . . . I ain't gonna lie. Leigh Stennis is a very, very comely young woman. I've always thought so, even when she first started to blossom. Now that her husband's gone, I could give her and her children a real good life." He paused. "I mean, she could do a lot worse than me."

"You think Leigh'd want you just for your money?"

Winston's hands gripped the arms of the leather upholstered swivel chair. He appeared to Kent to be at one second on the verge of making a clean breast of the matter;

and at another being mad enough to chew nails because he knew that he couldn't.

"It don't matter if she wants me or not . . . it's what I want that matters . . . And I get what I want."

Winston paused and cleared his throat. "Mackey, I don't know what you think you know, but you haven't got a case."

Now it was Kent's turn to take a deep breath. "Well, I know you threatened to throw Antonio in jail for passing bad moonshine, and you only kept him out if he'd kill Stennis.

"I know that Antonio told me that you threatened to arrest him for some imaginary rape of a white woman. He said you were gonna let your Klan buddies bust'im outta jail and hang'im." He paused. "Every man on the jury will know just how afraid Lincoln was of that threat.

"I know that Antonio tried to kill Thad Stennis twice: once over at Cyrus Roosevelt's house, and once on a car stop out on Number 9. Both times, he lost his nerve." He paused. "You know, that's what broke it. When I found out about Stennis's two close calls, and I realized from Toolen that you had engineered both of'em, well . . . ." He paused again.

"And, I know Antonio is expecting you to make all this go away."

"You can't prove any of that."

Kent took a deep breath. "I can prove enough."

"Well, you only think you can, but you don't have any evidence – against me." He paused. "And, you're forgettin' one thing."

"What's that?"

"That a white man's never been convicted of murder in Mississippi on the word of a nigra." He smirked. "Even if you manage to get a indictment, I'll beat it. Just wait'n see."

Kent said nothing for several seconds. He was a son of Mississippi and knew the good and the bad of its people, its customs, and its history. Mississippi's culture was his culture, for better or worse, and he knew that what Winston said was true – for now.

"Well, this time, I've got *two* black men, a white woman, and a bloody hammer, a bloody jacket, some money, and a back door that had to have been opened with a key." He paused and smiled. "Anyway, there's a first time for everything." He paused again. "Now, get up and get your shoes so we can go'ta town."

Winston paused and then leaned forward as if rising to his feet. Instead, he chose that moment to put his hand inside the desk drawer.

Kent instinctively knew that what Winston was reaching for was a gun. His own hand moved swiftly to his belt and in an instant his weapon was out and at the ready. Winston hesitated. Kent didn't know whether the Sheriff intended to use his gun on his self or on the two investigators, but when Kent saw the small revolver in the Winston's hand, he took no chances. He rose and, without hesitation he discharged one round in Winston's direction, striking him in the right shoulder. The Sheriff's gun went flying out of his hand and toward a fireplace, over against the side wall, and Winston fell out of his chair and onto the floor.

Nolen fumbled for the magnum on his belt and by the time the shooting was over, and Winston was grimacing in pain on the floor, the sheriff-elect had his gun in his hand and was around the desk and pointing it down at the injured man.

"Hold it, hold it!" Nolen said.

The noise of the handgun's report hung in the air. Kent smirked.

"Go find a phone and call an ambulance, Stew," he said to Nolen.

Nolen lowered his gun and tried to collect himself. "Oh, yeah, okay. I'll do that."

When Nolen was gone, Kent walked over behind the desk and looked down on Winston.

"You shouldn't'a done that Chet. You just hung a big 'guilty' sign around your neck." He nodded to the revolver lying on the floor near the fireplace. "I'd give you that piece back . . . if I thought you'd do the honorable thing." He paused and snorted. "Now's your chance. You can go be with Eva."

Winston's face was contorted in pain, but even so, he was defiant. "You son of a bitch. Don't you dare even speak her name."

Kent looked at him, hard, and silence settled over the room. In the midst of any homicide investigation, because the focus is on facts and forensic proof, a detective tends to lose sight of the human cost of murder. It must be ignored until the end, or at least until a jury makes an appearance. But as Kent looked down at Winston's face, a picture of a bloody and battered Thad Stennis came to his mind; then the image of Stennis' two fatherless children, as well as their house with its picket fence and red shutters, also intruded into his thinking. And at that moment, all the pain caused by Winston's lust, narcissism, even sociopathy, hit Kent like a brickbat to the face. Anger swelled within him, and he wanted to complete the work that the first bullet had left undone.

He looked down at Winston and spoke calmly. "You know what, you're right, Chet. You prob'ly will beat it." He paused and raised his gun toward the proud and haughty face of the man lying on the floor.

"So, in the int'rest of justice, I'm just gonna have to kill you myself – you arrogant bastard."

Winston's eyes widened in terror, and he raised his hands up in front of his face. "No, please," he whimpered.

At that moment, Nolen walked back into the room. Kent lowered his revolver and smirked.

"What's goin' on here?" Nolen said.

Kent shook his head. "Nothin'. We were just discussin' our options."

"Oh. Well, the ambulance is on the way."

Kent nodded. "Tell'em to take their time."

The End

Epilogue

Kent learned later that the blonde-haired man at Thad Stennis' funeral, the one driving the new Chevy Impala, the one that had stepped up to shake Leigh Stennis' hand, was an insurance salesman and that Stennis had just before the funeral taken possession of a ten thousand dollar payout. Without his wife's knowledge, Thad had purchased the policy right after he'd taken the job as deputy, just in case some how he was killed. Little did he know that he had nothing to fear from the criminals – it was his friends of whom he had the most to beware.

After Chester Winston's arrest, divers spent nearly two full days in the waters of the Missagoula River, but they were unable to locate either the knife or the courthouse key that Antonio Lincoln said that he had discarded into the muddy and murky waters. Kent was thankful that Jeris 'Red' Freeman had not been as judicious when it came to the abandonment of the hammer.

The blood on both Lincoln's and Freeman's coats turned out to be the same type as Thad Stennis; and with the blood, the money, the hammer, and the confessions Kent was able to put together an airtight case against the two men. In exchange for avoiding Mississippi's gas chamber, they both turned states' evidence, were sentenced to life in prison without parole – and testified against Chester Winston at his trial.

And with all the statements, confessions, and other circumstantial evidence, Kent was able to fashion a convincing contingent case against the Sheriff, and largely on the strength of Leigh Stennis' testimony, he was indicted for Conspiracy to Commit Murder by a grand jury empaneled in nearby Meridian, in Lauderdale County. Winston's attorney successfully argued for a change in venue, and his first trial was held there in June of '61.

In court, Lincoln testified to the fact that he had received one thousand dollars from Chester Winston to kill Thad Stennis; and Kent found evidence of a thousand dollar bank withdrawal from Winston's account at the Merchant's

Bank in Naomi some two months prior to the murder. Lincoln gave a one hundred dollars of the money to Jeris Freeman, and then proceeded to go through six hundred dollars in three days; primarily on a spree consisting of alcohol, gambling, and women. Kent and Nolen recovered what was left of the money, a little less than three hundred dollars, all in twenties, inside a Maxwell House coffee can buried in the well-kept flower bed next to the home of Alonzo Lincoln.

No evidence ever surfaced that Laura Leigh Stennis had an illicit relationship with Chester Winston. She, too, testified against him, telling the jury her story of years of sexual harassment; and even under the harsh cross examination by Winston's lawyer, David Holmes, the former Attorney General of Mississippi, she made for an unshakeable, therefore a compelling witness.

(It should be noted that afterwards, a few of the twelve male jurors remarked to the prosecutor that while they believed her, it sure took a long time for Leigh Stennis to realize her sense of outrage and discomfort with Winston's overtures.)

Most of the members of Winston's administration, the deputies, and also Margene Tyler, turned on him, and Kent was surprised to find out how many of them had actually observed the Sheriff's past advances toward Leigh Stennis. Those witnesses were helpful also; but due to their silence during the investigation they were somewhat less compelling.

At his second trial – the first jury found him guilty, but the case was overturned on appeal – Chester Winston was convicted again and was also sentenced to life in prison without parole. He died while incarcerated, at the age of sixty-seven, while maintaining his innocence to the end.

Antonio Lincoln died of lung cancer in prison in the 1970's; and Freeman deceased also, of natural causes, in the year 2000, at the age of 57.

Laura Leigh Stennis returned to teaching and eventually retired with a pension from the state of Mississippi. She never remarried. Her two children sued Wilcox County and also Chester Winston's liability insurance company for one million dollars in a wrongful death action. They settled out of court for fifty thousand dollars each and both used the money to attend Ole Miss.

Stewart Nolen asked Margene Tyler to remain on at the sheriff's department, and she did so. He hired four new deputies but retained the services Gil Toolen and Mark Ward. Nolen served his one term in office but spent almost the entire four years lobbying the state legislature to allow sheriffs to succeed themselves. The law was changed in 1966.

And Malcolm Kent continued working with the state police until nineteen eighty. He investigated many murder cases, and eventually wrote books about a couple of them. But in the quietness of his thoughts he reflected most often on this particular case both during the remainder of his career and for the rest of his life

It wasn't the most difficult murder investigation he had ever undertaken, nor was it the most dangerous. But it did turn out to be the only one he ever worked with a three thousand year old motive.

He often wondered if he would have actually shot Chester Winston at the time of his arrest had Stewart Nolen not re-entered the room. He eventually convinced himself that he wouldn't have; though he did want to. But in the end, he decided that by sparing the Sheriff's life he was giving Mississippi a chance to grow, Winston a chance to repent, and Laura Leigh Stennis a chance to mature with her reputation intact.

In the end, Kent found that lust, narcissism, and flattery will override good judgment every time; and really, there's nothing new under the sun.

FIN

Caleb Lott, who once was a homicide detective, is the pseudonym for the author who is a native of Mississippi and who now lives and writes in Alabama.

www.ingramcontent.com/pod-product-compliance
Lightning Source LLC
Chambersburg PA
CBHW031312060726

47590CB00003B/1183